A GUNSHOT AWAY FROM REAL TROUBLE!

LUKE TRAVIS: On Abilene's dusty streets, the tall marshal cut an impressive figure. He put down violence and kept the peace—with his powerful reputation or with a gun . . .

AILEEN BLOOM: The doctor, a woman of strength and compassion, cared for rich and poor alike. To save lives she would defy even Abilene's powerful ranchers . . .

CODY FISHER: Loyal, bold, and true, the young deputy stood by anyone in trouble—especially his own brother . . .

REVEREND JUDAH FISHER: Fiery and courageous as his brother Cody, he found his calling in the ministry and plenty of danger in the work . . .

HUNTER DIXON: Hard work and no mercy had made him Abilene's most powerful cattle rancher, a man who would crush anyone who threatened the open range . . .

ISAAC PARKS: The dirt-poor farmer was a newcomer in Abilene, but he expected justice for his people and a chance to make a living on the land . . .

B. W. ROYAL: With the flaming eyes and flowing beard of an Old Testament prophet, the bandit ruled his gang of hired guns. He loved to kill, and he had work to do in Abilene . . .

Books by Justin Ladd

Abilene Book 1: The Peacemaker
Abilene Book 2: The Sharpshooter
Abilene Book 3: The Pursuers
Abilene Book 4: The Night Riders

Published by POCKET BOOKS

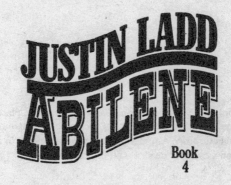

JUSTIN LADD
ABILENE

Book
4

THE NIGHT RIDERS

Created by the producers of
**Wagons West, Stagecoach,
Badge, and White Indian.**

Book Creations Inc., Canaan, NY · Lyle Kenyon Engel, Founder

POCKET BOOKS

New York   London   Toronto   Sydney   Tokyo

This book is a work of fiction. Names, characters, places and incidents are either the product of the author's imagination or are used fictitiously. Any resemblance to actual events or locales or persons, living or dead, is entirely coincidental.

Another *Original* publication of POCKET BOOKS

POCKET BOOKS, a division of Simon & Schuster Inc.
1230 Avenue of the Americas, New York, N.Y. 10020

ISBN: 0-671-64890-0

First Pocket Books printing October 1988

10 9 8 7 6 5 4 3 2 1

POCKET and colophon are trademarks of Simon & Schuster Inc.

Printed in the U.S.A.

THE NIGHT RIDERS

Prologue

Isaac Parks sat at the simple plank table in his family's rough-hewn cabin and stared at his gnarled hands, clasped tightly in front of him. The Georgia night outside the cabin was ominously quiet, the air heavy with the dampness of an impending storm. Isaac Parks was not brooding about the weather, however, but about another storm that was brewing evilly all around him.

Worry gnawed at the whole family. Isaac's wife, Hannah, moved around the table, serving a supper of fried chicken, potatoes, and greens, but as she placed the platters on the table she kept glancing nervously at the door and the window beside it. Across the table from Isaac sat his twenty-year-old son, Tommy, a frown creasing his haggard, lined face. The young man looked much older than his years, but then so did his parents. In one corner of the large room, the girl,

Verna, anxiously chewed her lower lip while she stood at the stove and stirred a pan of gravy.

Several hours had passed since the two carpetbaggers dressed in fancy suits had driven their shiny carriage to the Parks farm and informed the family that they would have to leave.

"It's all perfectly legal, Mr. Parks," one of the men had said with a smirk. "Your taxes on this land were due yesterday. You failed to pay them, so we've met that obligation and taken over the farm."

"But it's not right," Isaac had protested desperately. "I'm a law-abiding man, but the taxes have gone up so much. It's unreasonable!"

"It's the law," the second man said firmly. He was a fat man and was perspiring heavily in the humid Southern heat. He tipped his bowler hat back on his head and pointed the cigar he was smoking at Isaac. "You trash have to learn that you can't mess with the government. You had better be gone by tonight, or we'll put you off."

Tommy, who had been standing behind his father, had said angrily, "This is our land, and we're not leavin', mister. You try to put us off, and you're liable to get a bellyful of buckshot!"

Isaac Parks had seen the look of raw hatred that passed between the two carpetbaggers then, and he had wished that Tommy had been able to restrain his anger. These men were dangerous.

Without saying another word, the carpetbaggers had furiously whipped their team into motion, and the carriage had lurched down the narrow track in a cloud of red Georgia dust. With a sinking feeling—a deep, growing sense of foreboding—Isaac had watched them go. He had known that trouble would come. Some of his neighbors had tried to resist when the Northerners first arrived, and ugly violence and tragedy had been the result.

These thoughts plagued him now as he mechanically ate the supper Hannah had set before him. He fervently prayed that the hate that had ravaged the South after the Civil War would not touch his family.

The sudden pounding of hoofbeats shattered the stillness of the night and dashed his hopes.

At the sound of angry words outside the cabin, Tommy lunged to his feet. He snatched up the shotgun that lay on the bench beside him and took a step toward the door. Isaac moved quickly to stop him.

"Wait," he ordered his son. "I'll talk to them."

Hannah clutched at her husband's arm. "Be careful, Isaac," she pleaded with him. "Don't make them angry."

"I'll just tell them to go and leave us in peace," he told her, patting her shoulder. The war and its aftermath had been cruel, and Isaac had hoped to spare her any more anguish. She had been sickly for the last few years. He turned, opened the door, and stepped into the night as a man shouted his name.

Isaac Parks faced the terrifying sight of a dozen men on horseback. Several of them carried torches; others held rifles in their hands. The man in the lead grinned down at him and said, "Howdy, Parks. I thought you was told to get off this here land."

"Hello, Scobey," Isaac replied. His throat was dry and his voice cracked. He recognized the man as a local roughneck who would do just about anything, legal or not, as long as the price was right. The men with Scobey were cut from the same cloth, all of them hired thugs.

Isaac cleared his throat and went on, "This is my place. You've got no right to be here, and neither has that Northern scum you're working for."

"The law says different," Scobey replied, still grinning arrogantly. He jerked a thumb at the battered piece of tin pinned to the front of his dirty shirt. "I guess you didn't notice the badge. The fellas and I are special deputies now, appointed by the mayor."

Tommy strode through the open cabin door and stood behind Isaac. He still held the shotgun and started to raise it as he shouted angrily, "Get off our land, you dirty thieves!"

"Look out!" one of the men cried. "He's got a gun, Scobey!"

"No!" Isaac screamed. Seeing out of the corner of his eye that Scobey was reaching for the pistol strapped to his hip, Isaac whirled around. As the thug's gun cleared leather, Isaac grasped the barrel of the shotgun and forced it down, pushing Tommy out of the way.

Scobey's gun cracked.

A piercing scream burst from the cabin. Isaac jerked around, pulling the shotgun from Tommy's hands and flinging it to the ground. "You didn't have to shoot!" he exclaimed, staring in horror at Scobey. He turned toward the cabin door in time to see Verna dash outside, her hands covered with blood, her eyes wide with anguish.

Tommy grabbed the shoulders of the shaking, terrified girl and pulled her to a stop. "Mama?" he asked in a choked voice.

Verna shook her head. "She's hurt bad, Tommy,"

she stammered hoarsely. Tears streamed down her cheeks.

Isaac ran into the cabin. Behind him, he heard Scobey laugh and then shout, "Burn the place down! The new owner's got no use for a shack like this!"

Desperately scanning the room, Isaac's gaze fell on his wife. Hannah was slumped on one of the benches near the table. Her hands clutched at her middle, and blood flowed freely between her fingers. As she looked up at him, Isaac saw a trace of a smile on her lips. Then she fell on her side, and her eyes glazed over.

"Noooo!" Isaac wailed. He sobbed as he ran to her and gathered her limp, lifeless form in his arms.

Through the black veil of grief enveloping him, he heard Tommy's angry shouts, Verna's frightened screams, and the curses of Scobey and his raiders. A shotgun boomed; pistols cracked. A moment later, Tommy ran into the cabin, dragging Verna with him. He slammed the door behind him as bullets thudded into the thick, plank walls. The window beside the door shattered as slugs struck it, spraying shards of glass all over the room. A pair of torches flew through the opening, their flames igniting the faded curtains.

Tommy frantically clutched at Isaac's arm. "Come on, Pa!" he said urgently. "We've got to get out of here!"

The wooden walls burst into flame as Tommy tried to drag Isaac to the window in the back wall of the cabin. That window was their only hope of escaping death, for within moments the cabin would be an inferno.

As he stumbled toward the window, Isaac looked over his shoulder at his wife's body. The small part of his mind that was still rational knew Scobey's bullet had missed Tommy, gone through the open door, and struck Hannah. Grief overwhelmed the rest of his mind.

Tommy swiftly broke the window with the butt of the shotgun, smashing the glass several times to make the opening as large as possible. Then he helped Verna through it, being careful not to cut her on any of the jagged glass remaining in the frame. The young man urged his father through the opening next, then scrambled through the window himself.

A thick stand of pines grew close to the back of the cabin, and the three fugitives ran for the safety of the trees. Isaac could hear the raiders at the front of the cabin still shooting, whooping, and laughing as the fire caught hold and the simple building blazed.

As tree branches lashed at his face and body, Isaac Parks stumbled in the darkness for what seemed like an eternity. He knew he was leaving not only his beloved wife but all that he had worked for throughout his life. He was numb with shock. It was gone now, all gone—and it was all perfectly legal.

At dawn the next morning, Isaac Parks stood in the doorway of Fred Hoyle's cabin and watched the sun rise. Fred's cabin was two miles over the rugged hills from the Parks farm, and the three weary fugitives had found shelter there.

Isaac turned and looked into the cabin at the sleeping forms of Tommy and Verna. They had collapsed in an exhausted slumber that had overcome their grief and terror. Isaac had been awake all night, his mind churning, his heart broken. He sighed and looked once more at the brightening sky and Fred Hoyle's hard-won homestead, so like his own.

Seeing Fred chopping wood in a corner of the yard next to the barn, Isaac stepped through the cabin doorway and wearily walked over to him.

"Thank you for taking us in, Fred," he said solemnly as the neighbor leaned on his ax. "You know you might get into trouble yourself for helping us."

"I'll take that chance," Fred said. "Shoot, we're neighbors, Isaac. Neighbors got to help each other out." The man's mouth twisted in a scowl. "'Sides, they'll be coming for my place soon enough anyway. I can't pay my taxes, either."

"Why don't you and your family leave before that happens?" Isaac asked. During his sleepless night he had forced himself to think of a new life to avoid feeling his pain and loss. He knew other poor farmers in the area were experiencing the same problems he and his family had faced. In a very short time they, too, would be driven from their homes.

Fred shrugged. "It might not be a bad idea to make a new start, but where would we go?"

"I've heard of some folks who make it their business to help immigrants go west," Isaac told him. "They're some sort of religious society in Atlanta. I think we should all go talk to them, Fred. Your family, and what's left of mine, and all the other folks around here who've been losing their land."

As he put his thoughts into words, excitement grew in Isaac, and he began to plan even more. He and Tommy could go back to their farm and salvage what they could. Other families in the area might want to pack up their belongings, too. Isaac had a vision of a whole wagon train of his friends and neighbors, escaping the hell of a vengeful Reconstruction and heading west to a new land. Hannah would like that, he thought. She would like knowing that her family was going to survive and prosper with a fresh start.

He glanced at Fred and saw that his neighbor's eyes were sparkling as the vision Isaac had shared caught fire in him, too.

He clapped Isaac on the shoulder and said, "It sounds good to me. We'll go see those folks in Atlanta, all right. You think they can find us some land to farm out there on the frontier?"

"I'm sure they can," Isaac replied. "I've heard there's plenty of room in the West." For the first time in what seemed like an eternity, a smile touched his lips. "Some place like Kansas, maybe . . ."

Chapter One

———◆———

STANDING BEHIND THE MAHOGANY BAR IN THE IMMACU-
lately clean tavern that bore his name, Orion McCarthy placed his large hands on the cool hardwood and
leaned across its expanse to catch a little of the soft
breeze that blew through the batwing doors. The air in
the shadowy, low-ceilinged tavern was still and damp.
Outside the midday sun beat mercilessly on the hard-
packed earth of Texas Street. Abilene, Kansas, was
suffering through an unseasonably hot late-spring day,
and the heat punished the broad-shouldered, heavyset
Orion cruelly.

Shaking his head and scowling at his discomfort,
the burly Scotsman turned and glanced around his
tavern at his customers. His gaze rested on a group of
five cowhands playing poker and drinking beer at a
table in the back of the room, and his scowl deepened
into a frown. This sort of muggy day made some men

irritable and prompted them to do things they should not, and the men back there were the kind to look for trouble, Orion thought.

At the table, a slender, sandy-haired young man named Brice Dixon fanned out his cards and grinned broadly at his four companions. "Three pretty ladies," he crowed as he stretched his lean arms out and reached for the pile of coins and bills scattered in the center of the table.

The other cowboys muttered disgustedly as Brice raked in the money. "Reckon you're about the luckiest man I ever played cards with, Brice," one of them said.

"It's skill, not luck," Brice boasted. His tawny eyes narrowed slyly at the cowhand. "Hell, anybody could win playing against you boys."

The other cowhands furtively exchanged irritated glances, which Brice either did not see or chose to ignore. He knew perfectly well that no matter what they thought, these men would not get too upset over losing a few hands of poker to him—not as long as they were working for the Rafter D. Hunter Dixon, Brice's father, was the owner of the Rafter D, one of the biggest ranches in Kansas.

"You think your pa's goin' to be mad 'cause we didn't finish roundin' up them strays?" one of the men asked Brice.

Brice laughed and started to shuffle the deck of cards. "Those cows will still be there tomorrow. It's too damn hot to work today. A day like this was made for shade and cold beer." He swiftly dealt the next hand, expertly flipping the cards around the table.

Brice was dressed like the other men at the table, but his range clothes were newer and better kept, lacking the patches, frayed cuffs, and heavy stains of the other men's outfits. While Hunter Dixon expected Brice to pull his weight and work hard on the Rafter D, no one would ever mistake him for any hardscrabble, run-of-the-mill cowpuncher.

As the poker game continued, Orion moved up and down the bar, serving a few midday customers, mostly townsmen who had stopped in for a quick drink after lunch before going back to their own businesses. But Orion kept a wary eye on the five idle cowhands. Peels of laughter rang from the table where they sat, loud and genuine from Brice Dixon, a trifle forced from the other men.

Orion knew that Brice had been thrown out of most of the saloons in Abilene for starting fights. Hunter Dixon always paid for the damages, and the saloonkeepers usually relented and let Brice return. The young cowboy had never caused any problems in Orion's Tavern, but the Scotsman knew there was always a first time and was alert for any trouble. He hoped that the other Rafter D hands would keep Brice in line.

A tall, dark-haired young man pushed through the batwings and strode to the bar. A deputy's badge was pinned to his shirt, and a pearl-handled Colt rode easily in the well-oiled holster on his hip. The faint knife scar running down his cheek gave his handsome, lean face a forbidding, dangerous appearance, but a quick, friendly grin softened the impression. He placed a booted foot on the brass rail and leaned on the bar.

"Howdy, Orion," Deputy Cody Fisher said. "Hot enough for you?"

Orion's green eyes flashed, and his lips, almost

hidden in his full grayish-red beard, twisted in an impatient scowl. "Aye, lad, tha' it is. And I wish I had a nickel f' everyone who's asked me tha' question today."

Cody laughed heartily at his friend, then asked genially, "How about a beer?" As Orion bent to fill a mug from one of the kegs kept under the bar, Cody turned to scan the room, his gaze passing lightly over the patrons and pausing to linger on the five men engaged in the poker game. When he turned back to Orion, his dark eyes had narrowed in a speculative frown. He leaned toward the tavern keeper and dropped his voice. "Isn't that Brice Dixon back there?"

Orion shot Cody a glance that clearly expressed his unfavorable opinion of Brice Dixon. "Aye," he muttered.

"Figured Hunter Dixon would have him and those punchers out working."

Orion leaned closer to Cody and said in a hoarse whisper, "'Tis plain the lad does as he pleases, and those others go along wi' him."

"He causing you any trouble? I heard he got tossed out of the Bull's Head last week."

Orion shook his head. "No trouble. And I'm hoping it stays tha' way."

Cody lounged against the bar and sipped his beer appreciatively. Orion's place was not large or fancy, but it served the coldest beer in Abilene.

When he had emptied the mug, Cody set it on the bar with a satisfied sigh and slid a coin across the counter to Orion. "Reckon I'll head on back to the marshal's office," he said. "It's too hot for anybody to start a ruckus today."

"We kin hope," Orion muttered dubiously. As Cody ambled through the doors, Orion picked up a fresh towel and mopped the beads of perspiration from his forehead, then turned to look at the men in the back of the room.

At the table, Brice Dixon won another hand. Orion could see that his companions were becoming increasingly frustrated, but they appeared to be keeping their irritation in check. Brice neatly stacked the coins and bills in front of him, and once satisfied with his handiwork, he picked up his mug and drained it. Thumping the empty mug on the table, he called out, "Hey, Orion! We need some more beer over here!"

"Aye," Orion replied. He filled a pitcher from one of the kegs, carried it over to the table, and placed it in front of Brice. As he did, the thunder of a rapidly approaching horse pounded along Texas Street, drawing the attention of all the men in the tavern. Whoever was riding up was coming fast. The sound of hoofbeats stopped just outside the tavern, and a moment later bootheels rang on the planks of the boardwalk.

A dusty young cowhand slapped the batwings aside and strode quickly into the tavern. Removing his hat, he beat it against his clothes, raising a small cloud of trail dust. His eyes were wide, and he was visibly excited as he looked around the dimly lit tavern. When he spotted Brice Dixon and the other men seated at the table, he hurried over to them.

"Howdy, Brice," he said breathlessly. "Wait'll you hear what I just saw."

Brice, apparently in no hurry to respond to the new arrival, lifted the pitcher and poured himself a brimming mugful of fresh beer. Lounging back in his chair, he raised the mug and slowly drank it down. Then he turned his tawny eyes to the new man and said lazily, "You look a mite worked up, Monty. What did Pa have you doing today?"

"Mr. Dixon sent me over east of town with a bull he sold to the Rockin' M." The cowboy called Monty pulled out a chair and sank into it. "I was on my way back when I crossed the trail from Junction City. There was a whole wagon train full of settlers out there, Brice!"

Brice leaned forward and peered at Monty, a rare look of interest lighting his handsome face. "A wagon train? What are you talking about, Monty? There haven't been any wagon trains coming through here in a long time, not since the railroad was finished."

The other cowboys began to ask questions, too, but Brice cut through the chatter with a sharp gesture. He pushed the pitcher of beer across the table to Monty, who picked it up and drank directly from it. "Thanks, Brice," the young puncher said, licking his lips and wiping his mouth with his shirt sleeve. "That sure cuts the dust and makes talkin' easier."

"So talk," Brice said curtly. "Did you find out who those people were?"

"Sure," Monty replied with a grin. "There was some gals ridin' on those wagons, so naturally I stopped and asked who they were and where they were headin'."

"And?" Brice's features twisted in an impatient frown.

"Sodbusters. They was farmers, Brice, and they're headin' for Doyle Needham's spread."

Brice's frown deepened. "Needham's place? Why the devil would they be going to Needham's?"

"The way the old man who seemed to be in charge

was tellin' it, they're goin' to tenant-farm on Needham's ranch. You ever hear the like, Brice?"

Brice did not respond. He slipped into a brooding silence and considered the news as the other men started asking questions again. He knew Doyle Needham; he was the owner of a good-sized cattle spread west of Abilene. Needham's D Slash N was adjacent to the Rafter D. In fact, Doyle Needham, along with Hunter Dixon, had been one of the first ranchers to raise cattle in this part of Kansas.

Slowly, Brice's frown disappeared, and a mischievous grin spread over his face as an idea took hold. He did not care why the wagon train of settlers was heading for Needham's spread. What was important was the golden opportunity it presented to break up the boredom of a hot day.

"So, we've got some new citizens coming in, do we?" he said loudly, effectively stopping the conversations among the other men. "Well, we'll just have to give those squatters a good ol' Kansas welcome, won't we, boys?"

His grin was infectious. No cowboy worth his salt had any use for sodbusters. The men laughed and nodded in agreement as they pushed back their chairs and stood up.

As he sauntered past Orion, who now stood behind the bar, Brice dug in the pocket of his pants and drew out a double eagle, which he tossed to the Scotsman. Orion caught the coin deftly and watched with a worried look on his face as Brice and the ranch hands strode from the tavern. His frown deepened as he heard them mount up and gallop down Texas Street.

Turning to the young man who worked part-time for him, Orion said, "Keep an eye on the place,

Augie." He quickly untied his apron and slipped hastily from behind the bar.

Pushing through the batwing doors and walking onto the awning-covered boardwalk, Orion gasped as the full force of the heat struck him. He moved past the Sunrise Café with its gaily curtained windows and beyond to the Bull's Head Saloon, which he knew was decorated with gaudy paintings of plump nudes. Then stepping off the boardwalk and into the wide dusty street, he quickly crossed Texas Street and ducked back into the shade of the awnings. Only one carriage and two wagons moved along the street in the scorching sunshine, though normally it was a bustling thoroughfare at this time of day. Clearly, anyone who could was staying out of the heat.

With his destination steps away, Orion drew a clean handkerchief from his pocket and mopped the perspiration that once more drenched his face and beard. He stuffed the damp cloth into his pocket and pushed through the door of the marshal's office and jail.

As he entered, he saw that Marshal Luke Travis was in an uncharacteristically negligent pose. Travis's chair was tilted against the wall, and his booted feet were crossed at the ankles and propped on the desk in front of him. Through the open cellblock door, Orion could see Cody Fisher reclining on a bunk in one of the empty cells, his black hat tilted down over his eyes.

Orion, grinning broadly at the two men, put his hands on his hips and said, "Aye, 'tis a magnificent sight. The valiant guardians o' law and order, hard at work."

Travis looked up with a grin. He was a handsome, lean-featured man with sandy brown hair that was touched with gray at the temples and a mustache that drooped slightly over his generous mouth. He asked, "What can we do for you, Orion?"

"Brice Dixon and some o' his friends just left me place. They rode out o' town heading east, toward Junction City."

"He cause trouble in your place first?" Travis asked, his eyes brightening as his interest grew.

Orion shook his head no. Then his broad face twisted into a worried scowl. "He was ginna ride out t'meet a wagon train o' settlers coming this way."

Travis took his feet off the desk and let the front legs of his chair thump to the floor. "What wagon train?"

In the cellblock, Cody shifted onto one elbow and pushed his hat onto the back of his head.

"According t' the lad who brought the news, 'tis a group o' farmers heading for Doyle Needham's ranch."

"Farmers!" Cody exclaimed. He sat up and swung his legs off the bunk. "What would bring farmers to Needham's place?"

"I dinna know," Orion replied. "But 'twas plain t'me tha' Brice intended t'cause trouble for them."

Cody snorted as he stepped from the cell into the office. "Brice Dixon is full of hot air. I've never seen him start anything unless he had plenty of help and was certain all the odds were in his favor."

Travis stood up, his tall, well-muscled frame towering over the Scotsman. "Maybe so, but from what I've seen of Brice, he's liable to figure that a bunch of farmers would make a good target for some of his horseplay." He reached behind him and grasped the well-worn shell belt and holster that hung on a peg on the wall. The walnut-handled butt of his Colt Peacemaker protruded from the holster. "We'd better take a ride out there, Cody, just to make sure things don't get out of hand."

Cody mopped beads of perspiration from his forehead. "On a day like today, Marshal? How much mischief can Brice cause, anyway?"

"We'll find out," Travis replied dryly. "Like Orion says, we *are* the guardians of law and order." The marshal grabbed his tan, flat-crowned hat from the rack next to the door and walked out of the office.

"Thanks," Cody muttered to Orion as he stalked past the Scotsman.

"Always glad t'do me civic duty, lad," the saloonkeeper replied with a grin.

Chapter Two

T HREE MILES EAST OF ABILENE, A LONG LINE OF TWENTY rickety wagons crawled slowly, steadily across the scorching Kansas prairie toward the town. The canvas canopies covering the wagon beds were ragged and torn, showing the telltale signs of a long, arduous journey. A few of the vehicles were pulled by oxen, but most were drawn by teams of mules or horses. A handful of shabbily dressed men rode on horseback alongside the wagons.

Driving the lead wagon was a lantern-jawed, haggard man with gray stubble on his cheeks. He wore a floppy-brimmed felt hat, patched work clothes, and shoes that were threatening to come apart. Despite the weariness that drew deep furrows in his forehead and cheeks, his blue eyes flashed with interest as they scanned the dusty prairie intently.

Isaac Parks had led this band of exhausted people

hundreds of miles across the country in search of a new home. Now that they were close to their final destination, excitement and anticipation began to grow in him. It would feel good to be home again— even a new home.

Isaac's eyes narrowed as he spotted a dusty, hazy cloud moving toward them. The broad Kansas prairie was fairly flat, and he watched the cloud approach for quite some time before it resolved clearly into six men on horseback. As the riders drew nearer, one of the horsemen accompanying the wagon train galloped up beside Isaac's wagon.

"Somebody comin', Pa," the tall, rawboned young man announced.

"I know, Tommy," Isaac replied with a nod. "I saw them."

Tommy Parks leaned forward in his saddle. "Who do you reckon they are?" A Southern twang colored his voice.

Isaac's gaunt face creased in a smile. "A welcoming committee from Abilene, maybe?" he suggested to his son.

Tommy laughed, an unpleasant, jeering sound. "How many folks have been glad to see us since we left Georgia, Pa?" he asked cynically.

"Not many, I'll admit," Isaac agreed over the creaking of the wagon wheels. He tried to make his next words sound optimistic. "But I'm hoping it'll be different here in Kansas, boy. This is the frontier, the place where people can make a new start, build new lives for themselves."

"Yeah," Tommy Parks grunted sourly.

Taking his eyes off the approaching riders, Isaac shot a worried glance at his son. He was keenly aware of the bitterness in Tommy, a bitterness that had been planted long before Hannah was shot down. The Northern carpetbaggers had made life a living hell for the conquered Southerners. Not content to vent their smug anger on the big plantation owners, the carpet-baggers had pillaged and looted the common folks, folks who had never owned slaves and never desired to. Farmers who had wanted only to be left alone to work their land . . .

Isaac grimaced as a similar feeling of bitterness passed unbidden through him. White trash, that was what the carpetbaggers called them. Poor white trash.

But no longer, Isaac thought, defiantly refusing to yield to the ugly feeling, not out here on the frontier. They were in the West now, where every man had a second chance. Maybe those men up ahead had come to welcome them.

The sudden blast of shots, the puffs of smoke, and the sparks of flame that flared from the guns in the hands of the riders tore that hopeful notion from his mind.

"Dammit!" Tommy exclaimed, instinctively hunching over in his saddle to make himself a smaller target. "They're shootin' at us, Pa!"

Isaac hauled on the lines in his hand and wrestled the mule team to a halt. Behind him, he heard muttered curses as the other drivers did the same. Dropping the reins and scrambling to stand on the seat, he peered over the canvas top of his wagon and shouted to the people in the wagons behind his, "Take cover! Take cover!"

Tommy drew his skittish mount closer to his father's wagon. "Give me the rifle, Pa!" he demanded desperately. "I'll teach 'em—"

"No!" Isaac snapped angrily. "You'll just get yourself killed, Tommy." He looked at the shooting riders and went on, "They're not trying to hit us. Look!"

Firing their pistols into the air and whooping as they galloped toward the wagon train, the strangers were now within fifty yards of the wagons. Bandannas tied around their faces hid their features. Isaac, reaching cautiously into the wagon, grasped the breech of an old rifle. It would not hurt to be ready, he thought, just in case the attack suddenly turned more serious.

All along the wagon train, he heard the fearful cries of the children as the shooting, yelling riders swarmed around the wagons. The anxious women tried to calm the frightened youngsters, but they met with little success.

Isaac cast a worried glance at the wagon directly behind his as he heard its team of horses whinny nervously. Unlike the other wagons in the caravan, this one was not driven by a man. Instead, a young woman—not much more than a girl really—cowered on the seat, tightly clutching the reins and trying to keep the scared team from panicking.

The marauders swept past Isaac's wagon, forcing Tommy to yank his mount even closer to the sideboards to avoid a collision. There were only six riders, but the uproar they were creating made it seem as though there were many more. The man in the lead yelled at Isaac, "Welcome to Kansas, old man!"

Isaac shook with anger at the savage irony of the cry. As a rule, he tried to control his temper, but this arrogant, dangerous display made him want to raise the concealed rifle and start shooting—

"Isaac!"

The young woman's scream made him jerk his head around. As the strangers blasted slugs into the dirt around the hooves of her team, the panicked animals reared, stomped the earth, and then surged forward and off to one side away from the other wagons. The lines were wrenched from the slender fingers of the young woman, and the wagon lurched dangerously as the team bolted.

"Verna!" Tommy cried in alarm.

Isaac stared numbly as the runaway wagon careened across the prairie. He saw the dark-haired form of the young woman leaning over recklessly as she tried to retrieve the fallen lines. The wagon hit a bump just then, and the sudden jolt threw her down hard onto the floorboards.

"Verna!" Tommy yelled again. He dug his heels into his horse's sides and slashed at it with the reins in his hand. The horse responded instantly, and Tommy galloped at full speed after the runaway wagon.

A line of low bushes and trees stood a quarter of a mile away from the wagon train. Isaac's jaw tightened when he realized that the wagon was racing directly toward the trees. That hedgerow more than likely concealed a creek, maybe a gully of some sort, he thought.

He knew with a terrifying certainty that Verna's wagon would crash unless it was stopped before it reached the tree line. He had seen the twisted remains of men who had been injured in wagon wrecks, had seen what the grinding impact could do to a human body. He was equally certain that Tommy could not catch the careening wagon in time. Forgetting about the whooping, shooting strangers for the moment, he watched with horror as the terrible drama unfolded before his eyes.

"Verna," he whispered, unable to tear his eyes away.

Travis and Cody had ridden east from Abilene, following the Kansas Pacific railroad tracks and the trail from Junction City. With the baking sun and sweltering heat, the two lawmen had decided to travel at an easy pace, but the cracking of gunfire drifting through the hot air—more gunshots than would come from anything innocent—made them forget the heat of the day.

"Come on," Travis snapped, spurring his horse. Cody reacted instantly and urged his mount to a gallop.

A line of wagons came quickly into view in the shimmering air. Travis felt a surge of anger when he saw the masked riders circling the wagon train, firing their guns and shouting. He felt sure that Brice Dixon was under one of those bandannas.

Cody's horse pounded beside Travis's. "Over there!" the deputy shouted, pointing at a wagon that was bouncing crazily over the plains as its team raced frantically away from the shooting.

"See if you can stop it!" Travis commanded. "I'll handle those boys at the train."

With a grim nod, Cody steered his mount away from Travis and urged his pinto to greater speed. He was not sure if anyone was on board the runaway wagon, but then he caught a glimpse of a figure scrambling from the floorboards onto the seat. Long brown hair fluttered in the wind.

A woman! Cody leaned forward in the saddle and huddled close to his pinto's neck. He and the animal flew across the plain as he desperately strove to cut the gap between him and the careening wagon. Suddenly, he noticed another man on horseback, flailing his mount as he, too, pursued the wagon. Cody was closer, though, and if either man had a chance to stop the wagon, it was the young deputy. But if he did not bring the crazed team to a halt, Cody realized, the wagon would plunge into the trees ahead of it and crash.

Cody approached the path of the wagon at an angle, enabling him to cover the distance quickly. Once he reached the wagon, he swung his horse's head to the side to correct his course so that he was racing alongside it.

Glancing quickly toward the wagon seat, he caught a glimpse of tangled chestnut hair and young features set in a mask of terror. Despairingly, he spotted the reins dragging in the dirt, just behind the thundering hooves of the team.

As he looked ahead again, he realized with horror that the trees were less than fifty yards away now. Cody remembered from fishing trips that a narrow creek was just beyond them, and although its banks were not very high, the drop-off was abrupt. Should the wagon crash into the trees, the bank was steep enough to send the wagon cartwheeling.

Cody whispered soft words of encouragement as he tried to coax more speed from his mount. The horse could not have understood the words, but it must have sensed Cody's urgency because it responded. Reaching into its reserves of strength, the pinto gradually pulled past the wagon seat and drew even with the lead horses in the runaway team.

As his horse thundered beside the galloping team,

Cody took a deep breath. He saw only one sure way to stop the panicked horses in time. Leaning to the side in his saddle, he kicked his feet free of the stirrups, then launched into the air, flinging himself over the backs of the horses next to him. He spread his arms, his fingers frantically grabbing for anything he could hold.

In the same instant that one foot touched the wagon tongue, the fingers of both hands grasped, then twined in the manes of the lead horses. Cody hung on for dear life as the terrified animals wildly tossed their heads. He caught his balance and, one hand at a time, transferred his grip to the halters of the horses. Calling on all his strength, he hauled back heavily and slowed them. A moment later, they came to a halt, no more than ten feet from the trees.

Exhausted and breathless, Cody closed his eyes and did not move for a long moment. Taking in lungfuls of hot, dusty air, he coughed several times. Slowly he slid onto the back of one of the horses. Twisting around, he saw that the young woman driver was sitting on the seat with her face in her hands, her shoulders shaking as she cried.

Cody cleared the last of the dust from his throat and said hoarsely, "It's all right, ma'am. These horses aren't going anywhere now."

Before she could answer, the other man who had been chasing after the wagon came pounding up. He threw himself from the saddle, ran over to the wagon, and vaulted onto the seat. Clutching the young woman's shoulders, he said urgently, "Verna! You all right, Verna?"

Dropping her hands, she looked up, revealing large

brown eyes in a soft round face. Despite her tear-stained complexion and disheveled hair, Cody could see that she was a very pretty young woman. She threw her arms around the young man and clung to him desperately. "Oh, Tommy!" she cried raggedly. "I . . . I was so scared!"

Tommy put his arms around her protectively, patting her awkwardly as he tried to comfort her. He looked over her shoulder at Cody and said, "Don't know who you are, mister, but we're right thankful you came along. I've never seen anything like what you did."

Cody slid off the horse's back and said with a weary grin, "I never did anything quite like it, either. Seemed to be the only way to stop this wagon in time, though." He walked up to the wagon box. "I'm Deputy Cody Fisher, from Abilene. What the devil's going on out here, anyway?"

The young man turned abruptly and looked toward the other wagons. "Those . . . those men came ridin' up and started shootin'. . . . I got to get back!"

"Take it easy," Cody said soothingly as he started to walk to his pinto. "Marshal Luke Travis is over there. He'll put a stop to it if anybody can."

After Cody had swung his horse to chase the runaway wagon, Travis galloped toward the besieged wagon train. While he rode, he slipped his Winchester from the saddle boot and levered a cartridge into the chamber. Pointing the barrel of the rifle into the air, he squeezed the trigger.

At the Winchester's sharp crack, a couple of the marauders spun their heads around. They stopped firing. Travis heard them yell and saw them point at him to alert their companions to the approaching danger.

The six masked men wheeled their horses away from the wagons and put the spurs to them.

Travis bit back a curse as he saw the men veer north and race away from the wagon train. He fired a couple of shots after them, knowing he could not hit anything at this range from the back of a running horse. At least he had succeeded in driving them off. The wagon train was safe.

As the riders disappeared in the cloud of dust raised by their horses' hooves, Travis slowed his horse to a trot and slid the Winchester into its sheath. Then, cantering up to the lead wagon and reining his horse to a stop, he raised his hand in greeting to the tall, haggard man who stood on the wagon box clutching an old rifle.

"Howdy," Travis shouted to him. "Everybody all right here?"

The man turned toward the wagons behind him and called in a booming voice, "Anyone hurt?"

Slowly, negative replies came back to him as several men jumped from their wagons and hurried to the lead wagon. They clustered around it, clearly eager to learn what was going on.

"We appear to be unharmed, Marshal," the lantern-jawed leader told Travis. "Those men seemed content to fire into the air and scare us half to death."

"That's what it looked like to me, too," Travis agreed. "They were pretty quick to leave when things got more serious."

"When they saw you and your friend coming, you mean?"

"And when that team bolted." Travis shifted in his saddle and surveyed the prairie for some sign of the runaway wagon. To his relief, he saw it, undamaged, moving slowly toward the train. Cody Fisher rode on his pinto beside it. Travis was not surprised that the resourceful Cody had found a way to stop the team. His hotheaded young deputy usually managed to accomplish whatever had to be done.

Travis looked back at the wagon train's leader as the man said, "My name is Isaac Parks, Marshal. I suppose you could say I'm in charge of this group of pilgrims."

"I'm Luke Travis, marshal of Abilene," he said as he extended a hand to Isaac. "Sorry I can't welcome you under better circumstances, Mr. Parks."

Isaac Parks reached out and shook Travis's hand, then bent and placed his rifle in the wagon. As he straightened, he said, "Do you have any idea who those ruffians were, Marshal Travis, or what they wanted?"

"I've an idea who they were. Nothing I can prove, though, since I was not close enough to get a good look at them or their horses. As for what they wanted, well, I guess they were just having some fun at your expense."

Isaac grimaced. "Fun? Frightening innocent women and children? Stampeding a wagon and nearly killing a young woman? Can anyone think of that as fun?"

Travis nodded and said, "I agree with you, Mr. Parks, and I promise you I'll look into this, even though we are officially outside my jurisdiction. I figure anything that goes on in the area has an effect on the town of Abilene sooner or later."

One of the men standing in the cluster around

Travis and Isaac Parks blurted angrily, "You goin' to arrest them, Marshal? They oughta be throwed in jail!" Several other Southerners echoed his sentiments.

Travis took a deep breath and leaned on the pommel of his saddle. Looking sternly at the group, he answered firmly, "Just because I have my suspicions doesn't mean I can prove it. And I can't arrest anybody without proof, mister."

"I knew it," the man shot back bitterly. He turned his gaunt face to Isaac Parks. "It's just like ever'where else, Isaac. People don't give a damn 'bout po' folks like us."

"I'm sure that's not true, Henry," Isaac replied in an attempt to calm the man's outrage. "Marshal Travis is just trying to do his job." While the words were conciliatory, the tone behind them was less certain.

Travis's jaw tightened as he worked to control the mounting anger and impatience he felt. He and Cody had not hesitated to race in and help these troubled settlers, who apparently had encountered so many problems during their journey that they no longer trusted anyone, even those who intervened on their behalf. Making an effort to keep his voice level and polite, Travis asked Isaac, "Where are you folks from?"

"We've come from Georgia, sir," Isaac replied shortly. "And we plan to settle here." He looked past Travis at the runaway wagon as it returned to the train.

Following the man's gaze, Travis saw Cody on his horse next to the approaching wagon. A thin young man sat on the driver's box, holding the reins tightly, and a pretty but frightened young woman huddled next to him. Cody reined in beside the wagon as it came to a stop. Travis assumed the saddle horse tied to the back of the wagon belonged to the young man who was now driving.

"Are you all right, Verna?" Isaac asked anxiously.

The young woman nodded. She clutched the driver's arm as if she would never let it go. "I reckon I am," she whispered. "I . . . I was just scared."

"Damn lucky," the young man beside her growled. He nodded to Cody. "If this deputy here hadn't come along . . ."

Isaac turned to Travis and said, "Marshal, this is my son, Tommy. The girl's called Verna."

Travis touched the brim of his hat. "Glad to meet you. Like I was telling your pa, I wish it hadn't been this way."

"It won't be next time," Tommy Parks snapped. "We'll be ready for the bastards."

"Tommy! There's no need for that," Isaac sharply reprimanded his son. The gray-haired man took a deep breath and addressed the men gathered around his wagon. "Now that the danger is over, we'd best be getting on our way."

Muttering angrily about their welcome to Abilene, the disgruntled men walked to their wagons.

Travis found his anger and impatience dying as his keen eyes surveyed the caravan: the shabby old wagons, the torn canvas covers, the threadbare clothing of the travelers, the weariness in the expressions of the people. Thin-faced children peeped hollow-eyed at him from the shelter of the wagons. The gaunt women wore plain dresses and faded sunbonnets. Although many of them were probably still young, they looked washed out, drained of any vitality they might have once had. The features of the men were set in taut, angry masks.

Travis did not doubt that these grim-faced, proud people had seen a great deal of trouble. The Civil War had not touched him personally, but like everyone on the frontier, he had heard stories about the widespread devastation of the South. General Sherman's scorched-earth policy in the final months of the conflict had been bad enough, but then the assassination of Abraham Lincoln and the ineffectiveness of President Andrew Johnson had opened the door for all kinds of abuses. The South was under the heel of its Northern conquerors, and the carpetbaggers intended to see that it stayed that way.

Nevertheless, Travis wondered what had made them choose Abilene in particular as a place of refuge.

The wagons began rolling again. Tommy Parks worked the one he was driving into line behind his father's wagon as Travis turned his horse so that he rode alongside them. "We'll ride on with you for a while to make sure there's no more trouble," he called to Isaac.

"We'd be much obliged, Marshal," the man replied stiffly.

Cody moved up beside Travis, who glanced over at the young man and said, "Have any trouble getting that wagon stopped?"

Cody grinned and said, "Oh, not too much. Just had to jump on the team and rein 'em in."

"From horseback?"

"Yep." Cody's grin widened.

Travis shook his head. Cody was reckless, all right,

but he had stopped the wagon in time to prevent a tragedy.

As they rode, Travis decided to indulge his curiosity. In a carefully casual voice he asked Isaac, "What brings you to these parts, Mr. Parks?"

"Hope, Marshal," Isaac answered simply. "Hope and desperation." Isaac fixed him with an intense gaze. "Have you ever been to the South, Marshal Travis?"

Travis slowly shook his head. "Nothing closer to your part of the country than New Orleans," he answered. "And that was before the war."

"Then you have no idea how everything has changed there. That senseless struggle took so many of our young men, and on top of that, it ruined our economy. The . . . the whole structure of our lives was torn apart."

Travis frowned at the pained words. "I never held with slavery," he said.

"Neither did I. I never owned a slave, Marshal." Isaac's voice quavered. "But that didn't stop the carpetbaggers from burning my cabin and taking my land away from me . . . and killing my wife."

Travis raised his brow, clearly shocked by what the settler had said. "I'm sorry, sir. I . . . I know how horrible that is."

Isaac waved a hand to indicate the wagons following him. "All of these folks have had things like that happen to them. We finally got fed up with all of it and decided to pull up stakes. We figured there had to be a better place to live."

"So you came to Kansas."

Isaac nodded. "We're farmers, Marshal, and we're

good at it when we're given half a chance. I'm told Kansas has fertile land."

"That it does," Travis admitted. "What's that got to do with Doyle Needham, though?"

Isaac glanced at him in surprise. "You know that we're going to Mr. Needham's ranch?"

"The word's reached Abilene already. It's hard to keep too many secrets around here, Mr. Parks. Folks are always eager to hear the latest news."

Isaac frowned and said slowly, "A young man stopped by the train and talked to us for a while earlier today. I told him our destination. Could that have any connection with the men who attacked us?"

"It could," Travis said grimly. There was no longer any doubt in his mind that Brice Dixon and some Rafter D cowhands had been the masked men. But he did not share this with Isaac; instead he changed the subject. "You know that Needham's a cattleman, don't you?"

"He was," Isaac replied. "We've made arrangements to tenant-farm on his land."

Cody had been listening to the conversation with interest, and now he leaned forward and said incredulously, "You're going to farm on open range? String bob wire and plow up the grazing land?"

"Yes, Deputy. That's exactly what we're going to do."

Travis's eyes narrowed. "I'd heard that Needham had some trouble last year. . . ."

"He told me he lost most of his herd to disease," Isaac said. "Said it was Texas fever. That's why he was open to my suggestion that we farm the land. Now he won't have to worry about building his stock back up."

That was true enough, Travis thought, but if Needham intended to bring sodbusters in to farm on open range, the rancher was going to have plenty of other things to worry about. The older cattlemen hated few things more than barbed wire. Travis had heard that shooting wars had occurred down in Texas over the stuff, even though it had been introduced less than fifteen years earlier.

Farmers and "bob wire" . . . Luke Travis shivered as an eerie foreboding ran through him. But he said nothing as he rode beside the wagon train toward Abilene.

Chapter Three

———◆———

As the wagon train crawled at a snail's pace across the sweltering prairie, Luke Travis maintained a thoughtful silence. They had gone about a mile and were still two miles from the edge of town when he turned at last to Cody and said quietly, "Why don't you ride into Abilene ahead of us and let folks know we're coming?"

Cody shot him a questioning frown. "Are you sure that's a good idea, Marshal? After what just happened, I figured you might want to swing around town and go straight to Needham's place."

"These folks are going to be part of our community, Cody. They deserve a proper welcome, instead of what they've had so far. Pass the word to your brother, to Sister Laurel, and to some of the other citizens. It'd be a good idea to tell Orion and Dr. Bloom, too."

Cody nodded. "All right. I'll try to round up some

folks to make 'em feel more at home." The deputy spurred his pinto to a trot and rode away.

Isaac Parks called from the wagon seat, "I see you're sending your deputy ahead, Marshal. Do you think the people of Abilene will be happy to see us?"

The painfully hopeful look in the weary man's blue eyes touched Travis. He wished that he could guarantee a heartwarming welcome to this decent man and his followers, but he was well aware of the problems that would plague them.

"I can't speak for all of them, Mr. Parks," he answered honestly. "But I'm sure some of them will. Plenty of good people live in Abilene."

"I hope so, Marshal. We've experienced a lot of disappointments . . . many well before we began this trip. It would be . . . a pleasant change to feel welcomed."

Within fifteen minutes Cody had reached the outskirts of Abilene. He trotted past the Great Western Cattle Company Stockyards and slowed his horse to a walk as he moved down Railroad Street to turn south at Cedar. Dismounting, he slipped into Karatofsky's Store, the major mercantile in Abilene, then got on his horse again and turned the corner to head west on Texas, stopping at several of the stores that lined the town's major thoroughfare. At each of his stops he informed the merchants that a wagon train full of settlers was on its way into town, expecting the prospect of new business to spark their interest. Settlers always needed supplies, Cody pointed out to the businessmen.

"What do we need with a bunch of white trash like that in our town, Deputy?" one of the store owners said acidly.

Cody was stunned. "They looked like good folks to me," he replied coolly.

The bespectacled shopkeeper shook his head. "You don't have to do business with them and have them try to steal you blind, Deputy. I've had dealings with Rebels before. The government ought to make them stay there in the South. It's their fault the place is in ruins."

Cody clenched his jaw, turned abruptly, and strode from the store before he lost his temper. His mood worsened when he was greeted with the same reaction in about half the places he visited. He realized that Brice Dixon had spread the word that the settlers were from Georgia. By the time he reached Orion's Tavern, he was furious.

Orion looked up from behind the bar as Cody pushed through the batwings. "Ye look a wee bit red in the face, lad. 'Tis this heat. Kin ye use a drink?"

"You're right about the drink, but not about the heat," Cody told him as he leaned on the bar. "Has Brice Dixon or any of those Rafter D hands been in here in the last hour?"

Orion shook his head. "Dinna ye and Lucas find 'em?"

"Oh, we found them, all right, but they took off in a hurry." Cody then quickly described what had happened east of town. The Scotsman frowned and groaned when he heard about the attack on the wagon train.

"No one was hurt, ye say?" he asked.

"No, but it was just luck. I'm going to have to have a long talk with Brice real soon." Cody drained the mug of beer Orion had placed in front of him. "Those wagons will be here in a few minutes," he said as he thumped the empty mug on the bar. "Marshal Travis wants me to round up some of the townspeople to give these new settlers a friendly welcome. Why don't I meet you back here in fifteen minutes?" He strode toward the doors.

"'Tis a good idea," Orion called to him.

Cody nodded. "I'm on my way to see Judah, Sister Laurel, and Dr. Bloom," he said as he pushed through the batwings.

Leaving the tavern, Cody retraced his steps a few feet to the two-story cottage that housed Dr. Aileen Bloom's office. The small building was set back fifteen yards from the bustling boardwalk of Texas Street behind an attractively planted, well-tended yard. Bright spring flowers were blooming in front of the porch, lending an unexpected touch of color. Cody stepped onto the porch and opened the front door.

At the sound of the door opening, a slender young woman came into the front room, wiping her hands on the white apron she wore over her simple, tailored dress. Her thick brunette hair was swept softly away from her attractive face, accentuating her high cheekbones and warm brown eyes. She smiled brightly when she saw Cody standing in the doorway.

"Hello, Cody," Dr. Aileen Bloom said. "What can I do for you?"

Cody frowned at the crimson stains on Aileen's apron. "Looks like you've got a patient," he said, pointing to the red blotches. "I don't want to take you away from your work."

Aileen looked puzzled for a moment and then glanced down at her stained apron. Suddenly she laughed. "Don't worry, Cody, it's not blood," she assured him. "I'm cooking tomatoes to put up."

Cody shook his head and grinned sheepishly. "Sorry. I just thought . . . well, never mind that. Marshal Travis sent me to tell you that a wagon train full of settlers will be arriving in town in a few minutes."

Aileen's smile faded, and a look of concern replaced it. "Do they have medical problems?" she asked.

"Not that I know of," Cody answered with a shake of his head. "But they've come all the way from Georgia, and they've had a rough time of it. The marshal thought it would be neighborly for some of the townsfolk to get together and make them feel welcome."

"That is a good idea," Aileen said as she reached behind her and began untying her apron. "I think I should check to see if they have any problems that need my attention."

"That'd be just fine." Cody touched the brim of his hat and turned to leave. "I'm on my way to the church now to let Judah and Sister Laurel know." His grin widened as a thought struck him. "Those kids should be out of school by now, and I'll bet they'd enjoy watching that wagon train move through town."

With a wave of his hand he walked to the street and over to the hitchrack in front of Orion's Tavern. Untying his horse, he mounted up and rode west on Texas Street to Elm. Turning north, he followed Elm Street past Mud Creek and Hersey's old grist mill. A few years ago, a man had been lynched at the mill for killing another man, Cody remembered grimly. But folks no longer took the law into their own hands, he reflected, not since Luke Travis had come to Abilene and assumed the duties of town marshal.

On a small knoll overlooking the banks of Mud Creek, the whitewashed sides of the Calvary Methodist Church gleamed in the afternoon sun. Just beyond the church stood the parsonage where Cody's older brother, the Reverend Judah Fisher, lived. For several years Judah had lived there alone and wrestled with his private demons. But the recent arrival of Sister Laurel, a Dominican nun, and her boisterous group of orphans had changed everything for him.

Sister Laurel had left Philadelphia with several wagons full of children, ranging in age from toddlers to older teenagers, originally intending to establish an orphanage in Wichita. When the opportunity had arisen for them to stay in Abilene, Sister Laurel had seized it gratefully. She and Judah Fisher worked well together despite their religious differences, and now the orphans were housed in the Methodist parsonage. And Judah seemed to be thriving with their company.

Cody rode up the long curving drive to the front of the church and swung from the saddle. Looping the reins around the iron railing, he bounded up the four steps leading to the doorway.

Inside the simple, elegant white sanctuary, the air was cool. He walked slowly over the wide-plank floor, his booted footsteps echoing hollowly in the high-ceilinged church.

Judah Fisher, on his hands and knees beside the pulpit, was scrubbing the hardwood floor of the pulpit platform. A bucket of soapy water stood next to him.

As Judah looked up, Cody said with a grin, "I see you're doing the Lord's work as usual."

"Cleanliness is next to godliness," Judah said pointedly.

"So I've heard."

Judah dropped the rag he was using into the bucket and stood up. He was a tall, slender young man in his early thirties, a few years older than Cody, with piercing blue eyes behind black wire-rimmed spectacles. He brushed a lock of sun-bleached brown hair from his forehead and said, "I'm not going to comment about seeing you in church, Cody—that's a rare enough sight in itself—but what can I do for you?"

"The kids back from school yet?"

"I think so," Judah replied. "I believe I heard them return a little while ago. Why?"

"You think they'd like to come into town and greet a wagon train?"

"That sounds like something they would enjoy, all right. But a wagon train hasn't been through here in quite a while."

"There's going to be one today," Cody said. He repeated the story one more time.

As Judah listened intently to the plight of the settlers from Georgia, his expression changed from concern to anger. "Those poor people," he said sincerely when Cody had finished. "I'll certainly be glad to go down and greet them, and I'm sure Sister Laurel and the children will be, too."

"Better get moving, then," Cody said. "They ought to be here any minute."

Judah nodded and began rolling down his shirt sleeves. "I'll go tell Sister Laurel right now."

Cody mounted up as Judah hurried over to the parsonage. Turning his pinto toward town, the deputy noticed that from the little hill where the church was located he could see clearly across Abilene. The caravan of wagons was in plain sight now, less than half a mile from the edge of town. The wagons were rolling slowly but steadily down the trail, and within a few minutes they would reach the sprawling stock-yards of the Great Western Cattle Company.

He urged his horse to a fast trot and rode toward Texas Street. Should any trouble break out as the wagon train passed through Abilene, he wanted to be on hand.

As the wagon train crept into the eastern edge of Abilene, the sprawling two-hundred-fifty-acre stock-yards stood as a grim reminder of the troubles Travis foresaw for Isaac Parks and his followers. The cattle business brought not only prosperity to Abilene, but also trouble. Footloose cowboys, gamblers, and out-laws moved into prosperous cattletowns like Abilene along with the herds that were being shipped to the big markets. Travis and other respectable citizens had worked hard to keep the peace and make Abilene a good place to live. He knew only too well that many of those same good citizens would regard Isaac Parks and his band of settlers as a threat to their peace.

After mulling all this over during the trek into town, Travis decided to gamble on his lawman's well-honed instincts and prepare Isaac. "These stockyards should give you a good idea of why you may run into trouble here, Mr. Parks," Travis began carefully. "Cattle means big business in Abilene. A lot of people have built their lives around raising beef, and they don't want to see anything that will upset or change things. Some cattlemen around here won't like good rangeland being used for farming."

"Surely the things that our farms can produce are just as important as cattle, Marshal," Isaac said with a frown.

Travis shook his head. "Maybe so, but cattle and the railroad made this town what it is. The whole state owes a lot to the cattle industry. Once Texas ranchers like Charlie Goodnight and Oliver Loving proved what a market there was for beef, folks here in Kansas decided they wanted to raise cattle, too, instead of just shipping Texas beef to the big markets."

"But there have always been farms here, ever since the territory was settled, haven't there?"

"Sure," Travis agreed. "But I don't ever recall a cattleman switching to farming like Needham's doing."

Isaac sighed. "I suppose we'll just have to hope for the best, Marshal. That's what we've been doing for a long time now." His voice hardened as he went on, "I'm not the only one who's getting tired of being pushed around. We're not bad folks, Marshal. We just want to be left alone to live our lives."

"I hope that's just what happens, Mr. Parks." Travis sincerely meant what he said, but he doubted it would be that simple.

As the wagon train moved past the stockyards and onto Texas Street, Travis saw that quite a few people were already standing in clusters on the boardwalks. More citizens spilled out of the stores to watch the wagon train roll into town. Many of the men turned hard faces toward the newcomers, while the women inspected the shabby wagons with stern disapproval. The children were frankly wide-eyed with curiosity, especially when they noticed all the youngsters on the wagons.

The strange, uneasy silence that hung over the street bothered Travis even more than the stony looks the townspeople gave the Southern settlers.

Riding beside Isaac Parks's wagon, Travis felt confident that no one would start any trouble while he was there. He spotted Cody's horse tied to the hitch rail in front of Orion's Tavern and nodded a greeting as the deputy and the burly Scotsman stepped onto the boardwalk. Next door in the yard in front of Aileen's office, Judah Fisher and Sister Laurel had joined Aileen and were watching the wagons while trying to keep an eye on the excited group of orphans. Several of the children waved joyfully at their counterparts in the wagons.

A smile played on Travis's lips. Children did not care where you were from or how your folks made their living. They were much more interested in how well you could whittle or spit or roll a hoop.

At the sight of these welcoming faces, Travis signaled Isaac to halt the wagon train. He reined in and Isaac Parks pulled his team to a stop as Aileen, Judah, and Sister Laurel stepped into the street, meeting the newcomers in the center.

Travis leaned on the pommel of his saddle and grinned at his friends. Turning to Isaac, he said, "Mr. Parks, I'd like you to meet three of Abilene's finest citizens. This is Dr. Aileen Bloom, Sister Laurel of the Dominican order, and the Reverend Judah Fisher, pastor of the Methodist church. Folks, this is Isaac Parks, the leader of this wagon train."

Isaac doffed his battered hat and smiled at the three members of the unofficial welcoming committee. "I'm glad to meet you, ladies," he said in his deep, resonant voice. "You, too, Pastor."

"Welcome to Abilene, Mr. Parks," Judah said, stepping up to the wagon box and extending his hand to Isaac. "We hope you and your friends will enjoy living among us."

Isaac hesitated briefly. He drew a deep breath, then took Judah's hand. Aileen moved to stand next to Judah. "I'm a medical doctor, Mr. Parks," she said, "and I'd be glad to take a look at any of your people who are sick or injured."

"We're all fine at the moment, ma'am. We're pretty much used to taking care of ourselves."

"Yes, I'm sure you are. I just wanted you to know that my services are available anytime you need them."

"Thank you, ma'am," Isaac said, and he glanced back at the other wagons. "I'd introduce you to all the folks, but there's quite a few of 'em. We're a bit anxious to get to the Needham place, too."

"You can still get there by dark," Travis assured him.

Sister Laurel spoke up. "I'm sure we'll get to know all of you quite well, Mr. Parks. After all, you'll be part of the community now."

"I hope so, Sister."

While the gregarious Sister Laurel chatted warmly with Isaac, Travis casually scanned the street. The sullen crowd still stared at the Southerners, and the tension in the air had increased ominously since the wagons had stopped. Travis noticed his deputy lounging lazily against one of the awning posts in front of Orion's, but he knew only too well how deceptive that pose was. Cody was as ready for trouble as he was. Maybe Cody had been right when he suggested the train swing around Abilene.

But this has to be done sooner or later, Travis

thought. *These folks are going to live here. If there's going to be trouble, it will be better to get it out in the open first thing, rather than let it simmer only to explode later.*

Travis noticed that Judah Fisher was sweating, just as he was. The preacher knew the kinds of emotion that were lurking under the surface. Or maybe it was only the afternoon heat. As usual, Aileen Bloom looked cool and pretty, and Sister Laurel always managed somehow to tolerate the warmth of her heavy black habit.

Travis had accomplished his goal: He had brought the settlers into town and let them see that not everyone opposed them. Now the time had come to get them out of here.

"Go back to Georgia, you damn Rebels!"

Travis jerked his head around and glared at the crowd, trying to locate the source of the harsh shout. He saw a townsman step to the edge of the boardwalk and raise a clenched fist. Angrily shaking the fist at the wagons, the man went on, "You killed my boy at Gettysburg, you bastards!"

While some people on the boardwalk frowned disapprovingly at the outburst, several others echoed it. Nevertheless, once the jeering started, it seemed to feed on itself, and soon angry cries filled the air.

As Travis wheeled his horse, he noticed that Cody had abandoned his negligent pose. The young deputy was striding into the street, his hand poised near the butt of his Colt.

The Southern men on the wagon seats listened silently to the insults being hurled at them. Travis was certain that this was hardly the first time they had heard such abuse, for they made no move and showed no sign that they were affected by the verbal assault. But Travis knew men; he knew they would take this treatment for only so long. Then, humiliated in front of their wives and children, they would strike back.

"I'm so sorry, Mr. Parks," Travis heard Judah Fisher utter quickly to Isaac. He shook his head sadly as more ugly words poured from the citizens of Abilene.

Slowly Travis rode down the center of Texas Street along the train, his furious gaze raking over the jeering townspeople. Some of the men who had been yelling fell silent as he passed them. Travis singled out the man who had begun the shouting and rode directly up to him.

Travis thought he looked vaguely familiar, but he did not know the man's name. Glaring at the man's flushed face, he snapped, "You got anything else to say, mister?"

The red-faced man tightened his jaw. As he glowered at Travis, the shouting along the street slowly died away. The townspeople and the Southerners were focusing on the confrontation between Travis and the angry man, just as Travis had hoped they would.

"You're damned right I've got something else to say, Marshal," the man finally growled. "You goin' to let me say it, or are you just interested in protectin' these Rebs?"

"The law says a man's got the right to talk as much as he wants," Travis answered coldly, "whether what he says makes sense or not."

"I'm makin' sense, all right." The man raised his voice and turned to address the people gathered on the boardwalk. "Why the hell do we need a bunch of dirt-poor Rebel trash draggin' our town into the mud? Did you ask 'em to come? Did you?"

As he spoke the man singled out two bystanders and angrily pointed a quivering finger at them. Both men shook their heads vehemently.

Cody stalked up and stood between the man and the crowd. His dark eyes stared grimly as he said, "Did anybody ask you to come here, mister, or did you just show up looking for a better place to live?"

"I came on my own," the man replied haughtily. "I've always done things that way. Never asked for anybody's help."

Cody waved an arm at the wagon train. "Neither are these folks. They just want a chance to make a life for themselves. They're not going to get that in the South."

Travis was proud of Cody for speaking up, but he knew it would not do much good; the old attitudes were too ingrained.

Travis stared at the man who had started this commotion and said levelly, "I don't care what you think about these folks. I can't change that. But while they're in my town, they'll be treated lawfully and decently. You understand that, mister?"

After a moment, the man nodded grudgingly. He muttered, "I just want 'em to go back where they came from." He turned and stormed down the boardwalk. As he passed, the silent bystanders moved aside to let him through.

Travis watched with satisfaction as the crowd along the street began to disperse. He had defused the situation by confronting the man who had brought it into the open. He realized that the angry feelings underlying it still existed, and that tough talk would not drive them away.

Glancing at Cody, Travis said, "I think I'd better ride out to Needham's place with these folks. You keep an eye on things here in town while I'm gone, all right?"

Cody nodded. "Sure, Marshal."

"And if you see Brice Dixon, tell him I want to talk to him."

Cody's lips twitched as a slight smile played over his face. "I'll tell him," he said. "Be glad to."

Travis hesitated, wondering what Cody intended to do if Brice Dixon ventured into Abilene. Then he shrugged and rode toward Isaac's wagon. Cody was a lawman, Travis thought. He might not always follow the book, but he would not stray too far.

As he passed the second wagon in line, Travis noticed the tension on Tommy Parks's face. Taking his measure of the young man, Travis sensed that Tommy would not take much abuse before he struck back. The marshal would remember that.

Judah, Aileen, and Sister Laurel were still apologizing to Isaac, assuring him that not everyone in Abilene opposed the settlers, when Travis rode up. "I appreciate what you tried to do, folks," Isaac was saying, "but I reckon we'd best be moving on. Given a little time, maybe things will quiet down later."

He flicked the reins and shouted at his mules. The team began moving slowly. Travis glanced at Aileen Bloom, and he saw the tense, worried look on her face. Only a fool would feel optimistic after this episode, he thought, and Aileen was no fool.

The wagon train rolled down Texas Street and out of Abilene, the wheels of the vehicles clattering on the bridge over Mud Creek. Travis knew the way to Doyle Needham's D Slash N, and several miles west of town, he directed Isaac Parks to swing his wagon train to the northwest.

The sun was lowering toward the horizon, bathing the hot Kansas prairie in an orange glow, when Travis spotted Needham's ranch house. The white, two-story frame building stood on a knoll surrounded by trees. Needham had built the house for his wife, Travis recalled, and had lived there alone ever since the woman had passed away several years earlier. A long, low bunkhouse sprawled a hundred yards beyond the ranch headquarters. A barn surrounded by several corrals loomed next to the bunkhouse. At one time, the D Slash N had been a well-run, prosperous ranch, but now the corrals were simply fences around open land, housing nothing, and the bunkhouse appeared to be empty, too. Needham must have let his hands go after Texas fever had decimated his herd.

Isaac led the wagon train directly to the house, pulling his wagon to a halt in front of it. The door banged open, and Doyle Needham strode onto the shaded porch. Travis had met him a few times in Abilene but did not know him well. Needham was a wiry man just under medium height. His dark hair was shot with gray, as was the thick mustache he sported. He hooked his thumbs in his belt and looked up at Isaac, who was still sitting on the box of his wagon.

"You must be Parks," Needham said curtly.

"I am." Isaac nodded. "I'm glad to meet you after all the letters we've exchanged, Mr. Needham."

"Expected you before this." Needham switched his gaze to Travis. "What are you doing out here, Marshal?"

"There was some trouble," Travis answered without offering any further explanation. "I want to talk to you, Needham."

"So talk."

"Hadn't you better get these folks settled in first?"

Needham nodded impatiently. "Sure, sure." He turned to Isaac and said, "Just drive the wagons on down to the bunkhouse. Your people can stay there for a while until we decide who's going to farm which section of land. I expect you'll want to put up your own soddies then."

"That's fine, Mr. Needham," Isaac said. "I suppose we can use your corrals for our stock?"

"Right." Needham stood on the porch and watched as the wagons rolled around the house and headed for the bunkhouse. When the last one was bounced away, the rancher turned back to Travis and snapped, "Now what the hell do you want with me, Marshal?"

Travis did not dismount, and Needham did not ask him to. The marshal said, "I hope you know you're going to have trouble over this, Needham."

"From you? I ain't broken no laws."

Travis shook his head. "I don't care if you run cattle or farm or dig for gold out here, Needham. But the other cattlemen and a lot of the people in Abilene won't see it that way. It's not just that you brought in a whole group of poor settlers, although Lord knows that'd be enough to set some folks off. It's this business of giving up ranching and turning to farming. You know the other cattlemen aren't going to like that."

Needham snorted contemptuously. "I don't recollect any of them runnin' over here to help me when my stock was dyin' right and left."

"Maybe not, but they've got no use for farmers and barbed wire. They're used to open range. They're going to consider you a turncoat."

"It's my land, and I'll do what I want with it," Needham bristled. "And I'll take a gun to anybody who tries to tell me different."

Travis sighed. He had expected this response from Doyle Needham. Needham's abrasive personality was well known. He had never gotten along well with his neighbors, particularly Hunter Dixon, whose spread bordered Needham's to the north. Now, to Dixon and the other ranchers, Needham was just another sodbuster to be trampled if need be.

"You get in touch with me if you have trouble," Travis warned.

Needham laughed harshly. "I've always handled my own problems, Marshal. That ain't goin' to change now."

Travis nodded. He could see that more talk was not going to do any good. He wheeled his horse and walked his mount away from the ranch.

As he rode down the trail away from the ranch house, he paused and looked back at the buildings. The settlers were unloading their wagons and moving some of their belongings into the D Slash N bunkhouse. The children were running around the yard playing a game, and Travis could faintly hear their laughter. They probably felt they had finally reached their new home.

For the sake of the children, Travis hoped they were right.

Chapter Four

AT DAYBREAK THREE MORNINGS LATER AS ORION MC-
Carthy sat drinking his coffee, he finally made the
decision to ride out to the Needham ranch. The clear,
bright dawn held the promise of a beautiful spring
day, and he had nothing earth-shattering to attend to
in Abilene. What was driving him was the memory of
the welcome Abilene's citizens had given the Southern
settlers. The image of those impoverished people
sitting on their wagons as they were harassed by the
more prosperous townspeople enraged him.

He had hoped Isaac Parks would come into town on
some errand so that he could tell the man how he felt
and perhaps rectify the ugly impression of Abilene
Isaac must have. But none of the settlers had ventured
into town during the past three days.

Orion decided he would seize the initiative. Waking
Augie and telling him to mind the tavern, he mounted
up and was on his way long before seven.

Doyle Needham was in his house when Orion came riding up on a big bay horse. The rancher must have heard the saloonkeeper's approach, because he strode onto the porch with his right hand resting on the butt of the pistol holstered at his hip. He frowned at Orion and snapped, "McCarthy, ain't it? What the hell are you doin' out here?"

Orion pushed back his broad-brimmed hat and gazed around the yard. He saw no wagons parked anywhere, and the corrals held only a couple of old milk cows. A saddle horse was tied to one of the porch rails.

"I come t'see tha' fellow Isaac Parks," Orion said. "D'ye know where I might be finding him?"

Needham kept his hand on his gun. "What's your business with Parks?" he demanded.

"Tha' be a'tween him and me," Orion replied. He had never liked Doyle Needham, and the rancher was giving him no reason to revise his opinion now.

Another man came out of the house, and Orion recognized the tall, gray-haired figure. "I'm Isaac Parks," the man said as he came down the porch steps. "What can I do for you, friend?"

Orion leaned over in the saddle and extended his hand. "Orion McCarthy," he introduced himself. "I be the proud proprietor o' Orion's Tavern in Abilene."

While Needham looked on suspiciously, Isaac shook Orion's hand and said, "I remember seeing your establishment, sir. I believe you mentioned you had business with me."

"Aye. Lucas—tha' be Marshal Travis—told me tha' ye intend t'farm this land. Ye'll be putting up soddies, will ye not?" Orion asked, referring to the houses built from strips of cut turf. The dwellings were not unusual here on the plains, where timber was hard to come by.

Isaac nodded. "Indeed we will. In fact, we've already started building them. That's where everyone is now."

"Not that it's any of your business, McCarthy," Needham put in harshly, "but we've spent the last couple of days decidin' which family is goin' to farm which section. You can tell Travis everything is fine. I reckon he's the one who sent you out here to spy on us."

Anger surged inside Orion, and he repressed it with effort. Ignoring Needham's gibe, he told Isaac Parks, "I come t'offer me help, Mr. Parks. I've put up a few soddies in me time."

Isaac smiled. "In that case, you're more than welcome, Mr. McCarthy." He untied the other horse and swung into the saddle. "You can come with me to our place." Calling to the rancher, he said, "I'll see you later, Mr. Needham."

Isaac turned his mount and trotted away from the house. Orion shot a parting glance at Doyle Needham, who still glowered hostilely, and then the Scotsman followed the leader of the settlers.

As Orion came up beside Isaac, the gray-haired man looked at him and said, "I'm afraid Mr. Needham doesn't have much use for anybody from Abilene."

"From wha' I've seen o' him, Needham's got no use f'anyone. An unpleasant man he is, Mr. Parks."

Isaac laughed shortly. "I guess I have to agree with you, Mr. McCarthy. But he has good land, and he's willing to let us use it for our farms. We're grateful to him."

"Call me Orion."

"All right, Orion. I'm Isaac."

The two men rode over the plains in silence for a few minutes. The gently rolling prairie so common in this part of the country was punctuated with occasional clumps of trees, pastures of thick grass, and patches of wildflowers beginning to bloom. The sweltering heat of a few days earlier had abated, leaving the air pleasantly warm and fragrant with spring.

Orion noticed a rise ahead of them, and against the side of the shallow hill were the beginnings of a sod dugout. Blocks of earth had been cut and laid out to mark the foundations for three walls, the hill serving as the fourth wall. More chunks of sod would be stacked up to form the walls themselves. With the scarcity of timber on the prairie, only people with quite a bit of money could afford a frame house. For poor settlers like Isaac Parks, soddies would have to do. The few planks they could acquire would be used as roof supports for the earthen cabins.

Two wagons were parked next to the foundation of the soddy, and Orion saw a young man and woman hard at work. He recognized them from the wagon train's passage through Abilene and knew from what Travis had told him afterward that they were Isaac's son, Tommy, and a young woman called Verna. Travis had been uncertain of Verna's relation to Isaac and Tommy, although he said she seemed to be treated as part of the family.

Tommy looked up as Isaac and Orion approached the wagons. He brushed his face with his sleeve to wipe away the dirt and sweat. He had been stacking the heavy blocks of sod, and he was breathing heavily from the exertion. His lean face wore a wary expression as he appraised Orion.

"Who's this, Pa?" he asked in a surly voice.

Isaac dismounted, a stern frown on his face. "That's no way to greet a visitor, Tommy. This is Mr. McCarthy from Abilene, and he says he's come to help us with the soddies."

"Why would you want to do that, McCarthy?"

"I saw wha' happened when ye came into town, lad. Reckoned ye should know tha' not all the folks o' Abilene be agin ye." As he spoke, Orion smiled at Verna. The pretty young woman stood shyly behind one of the wagons and peered uncertainly at the big Scotsman.

Tommy looked unconvinced. He shrugged and turned to his father. "Did you and Needham settle that business?" he asked.

Isaac nodded. "Yes, he agreed that the Logan family needs more land to support themselves, what with those twelve children. We adjusted the original division of land. I'll ride over and tell the Logans later." He swung down from the saddle and began to roll up his shirt sleeves. "Right now I suppose we should get to work."

Orion grinned and pushed up the sleeves of his shirt on his muscular forearms. "Tha' be just wha' I was thinking," he said as he dismounted.

Several squares of earth were stacked near the dugout. Orion hefted one and carried it to the wall opposite the one where Tommy was working. Carefully positioning it on top of the first layer, he pressed it down to secure it in place, then returned for another piece of sod. Isaac Parks did the same on the front wall. Verna returned to her job. She was cutting out the chunks of earth with a plow pulled by an ox. It was hard work, but Orion noticed that she performed it without complaint.

The day grew hotter as the sun rose higher and higher in the sky. By noon, Tommy had removed his shirt, and the others were drenched with sweat. But the work had gone much faster with three men, and the sides of the soddy were almost complete. Isaac called a halt and said, "You'll be staying to eat with us, I hope, Orion."

"Aye. 'Twould be me pleasure."

The meal was simple fare: beans, biscuits, and canned tomatoes. Tommy's attitude had softened once he saw how hard Orion was working, and now as he lifted one of the juicy chunks of tomato with his fingers, he said warmly to Orion, "Next year we'll have our own tomatoes, grown right here."

"Aye, I reckon ye will," Orion replied with an easy smile. "'Tis good land."

Isaac nodded as he chewed on a biscuit. When he was finished, he knelt and picked up a handful of the soil, rubbing it between his fingers. "A man can tell that just by looking at it and touching it," he said. "Given time, we can make a paradise out of this country, Orion."

The Scotsman laughed heartily. "I dinna know about tha'. 'Twill still be Kansas, not paradise. But 'twill make a good farm, right enough."

"That's all we ask," Isaac said.

Verna had prepared the meal and eaten with them, but she had said nothing. Now she looked up from her battered tin plate and said wistfully, "I still miss Georgia."

"I know you do," Isaac replied softly. "And I do,

too. But this is our home now, and we have to make the best of it."

"Going to be hard, the way the folks in Abilene feel about us," Tommy said. "They don't want nothing to do with us."

"They don't want *anything,* Tommy, not *nothing."* Isaac nodded toward Orion. "What about Mr. McCarthy here? Nobody made him come out here to help us, Tommy. He did it because he wants us to feel welcome."

"And so ye'll come into me place from time t'time for a drink," Orion added with a broad grin.

Isaac smiled. "I'm afraid I don't hold much with drinking, but there are plenty of men in our group who like a little nip now and then. I'm sure they'll patronize your tavern, Orion."

"Best whiskey in Kansas," Orion boasted. "'Twill make ye friends forget their Georgia corn liquor."

That brought a laugh from Isaac and smiles from Tommy and Verna. "I doubt that, Orion," Isaac said. "I seriously doubt that."

They went straight to work after the meal, and by midafternoon the sod dugout was complete. Now Isaac and Tommy could finish unloading their belongings from the wagon.

Orion slapped the solid wall of the soddy. "'Twill be cool in the summer and warm in the winter, and if ye be lucky, 'twill not rain too much in between. These soddies have a tendency t'leak a mite."

"I'm sure it'll be fine," Isaac said with a warm smile. He extended his hand to Orion. "You have our thanks, Mr. McCarthy."

"And ye be mighty welcome," Orion replied, shaking Isaac's hand. "Now, if ye'll show me the way to the next cabin, I'll see if I kin give the folks a hand wi' it."

"I'll do better than that. I'll take you and introduce you around to our people. I'm sure they'll appreciate a visit from a friendly face."

Orion and Isaac both took drinks of cool creek water from the bucket Verna had filled at a nearby stream. Then they mounted up and rode out, leaving Tommy and Verna to complete the unpacking. Orion's back and shoulders ached as he rode, but it was a good feeling.

He had helped these people, and maybe today would mark the beginning of their acceptance in the community.

Luke Travis was surprised that the last three days had passed so uneventfully. No more trouble had erupted between the townspeople and the settlers from Georgia, but upon reflection, Travis realized that the settlers had stayed pretty close to Needham's ranch, thereby eliminating the possibility of a conflict.

He had planned to go out to the spread early that morning, for he had not visited the settlers since the day they had arrived, but by the time he had sorted out the other matters that distracted him, it was afternoon.

As he walked his horse down Texas Street toward the western edge of town, he spotted Aileen Bloom, climbing into her buggy, which was parked at the boardwalk in front of her office.

Travis reined in and lifted a hand to the brim of his hat. "Afternoon, Aileen," he said. "Going out on a call?" He noticed that she was carrying her black medical bag.

"Not exactly," the doctor replied. She settled herself on the buggy's seat and smiled at him. "I thought I'd take a drive out to Mr. Needham's ranch and check on those folks from Georgia. I know Mr. Parks said that they didn't need any medical attention, but he was in a hurry to get the wagon train through town at the time."

"You think maybe some of them are sick?"

Aileen shook her head. "Oh, I doubt there's anything serious, but I'd especially like to take a look at the children. So many things can go wrong during a long trip like the one they made, being exposed to the elements so much."

"Well, I don't know how welcome they'll make you feel. Just remember that those folks can be standoffish. I'm on my way out there now, and I'd be glad to ride with you."

Aileen smiled and said, "Yes, I'd enjoy having your company, Luke."

She took up the reins and expertly steered the buggy away from the boardwalk and down Texas Street. Travis walked his mount alongside the buggy, trying not to grin too broadly as Aileen chatted brightly with him.

Travis enjoyed the doctor's company, and he knew she liked being with him, too. She certainly looked lovely in the clear afternoon sunshine. Dressed in a simple, dark blue suit, a hat of the same shade was perched on her deep brown, upswept hair. From the first time he had met her, Travis had been impressed with Aileen Bloom's beauty. As he had gotten to know her better, he had also come to admire her intelligence, courage, and determination. Aileen was special, and Travis had told himself more than once that Abilene was lucky to have her practicing there.

"Has there been any more trouble between the townspeople and the settlers?" Aileen asked as they rode toward Needham's D Slash N. "I haven't heard about anything, but you'd know more about that sort of thing."

"Everything's been quiet," Travis told her with a shake of his head. "I've been telling myself just to hope that it stays that way, but I'm not convinced it will. The feelings run too deep to go away quickly. As long as those Southerners stay out of town as much as possible, maybe we can keep things under control."

Travis and Aileen went first to Needham's ranch house. The former cattleman stalked onto his porch and greeted them curtly, clearly annoyed by the intrusion. "Saw that fella McCarthy out here earlier today," Needham went on. "I figured you sent him, Marshal."

"I'm looking for him myself," Travis said. "Do you know where he went?"

"He left here with Isaac Parks." Needham jerked a thumb toward the northwest. "You might try the section that Parks is going to farm. It's about a mile and a half that way."

"Much obliged. Is it all right with you if Dr. Bloom pays a visit to some of the settler families?"

"That's none of my business," Needham snapped. "Just remember, Travis, I ain't responsible for anything that happens while you're here. If you run into trouble, it's your own business."

Travis grimaced. "Have there been any problems?"
Needham shook his head. "Nope, but I reckon

Dixon and the others have all heard about what I'm doing with these sodbusters. I had to let all of my hands go, so I'm not really sure what's happenin' out on the range."

"We'll find out," Travis said grimly. He turned his horse and rode out of the ranch yard. Aileen drove the buggy beside him. He was not worried about encountering any cowboys from the neighboring spreads. As upset as they might be about Needham's switch to farming, Travis was confident they would not bother Aileen and him.

When they reached Isaac Parks's soddy, they saw Tommy and Verna carrying things into the dugout from the wagons. Travis was a little surprised to see that the earthen cabin was finished.

He reined in and nodded, saying, "Howdy, Tommy. Ma'am." He touched his hat as he greeted Verna, who looked a little bewildered and embarrassed by his politeness. Turning back to Tommy, he explained, "I'm looking for my friend Orion McCarthy. He's a big Scotsman with a beard—"

"I saw him," Tommy cut in. "Fact is, he and my pa just left here a few minutes ago. McCarthy helped us finish the soddy today."

Travis nodded and smiled. He had wondered if Orion had come out here to lend a hand to the settlers. That was the kind of thing Orion would do.

While the men spoke, Aileen noticed that Verna was lifting a small wooden chest from Isaac Parks's wagon. Climbing down from her buggy, the doctor moved to give the young woman a hand. She grasped one end of the little chest and was surprised that it was heavier than it looked. Carrying her end of the burden, she followed Verna into the soddy.

After they had crossed the threshold, Verna said, "Let's set it down on that trunk."

The two women placed the chest on a long, heavy trunk. Aileen let her fingertips trail over the wood of the small chest, which had been lovingly polished to a high shine. A brass latch held the lid in place. "This is a lovely piece. It looks old."

"It is," Verna said. "My great-grandpa made it, 'fore he died at the Battle of New Orleans."

"That was a long time ago."

"Yes, ma'am." Verna unfastened the latch and lifted the lid. Inside was a massive book with thick leather bindings. "This here is our family Bible," she said softly. "It come down to me from my great-grandpa, just like this box he made for it."

Aileen caught her breath. "Would it be all right if I looked at it?"

Verna hesitated, then said, "Well . . . I reckon it'd be all right."

Aileen reached out and lightly ran her fingers over the leather bindings. Then she gently lifted the front cover. The pages were thick vellum, and the legend at the bottom of the title page read "Townsend and Sons, Printers, Philadelphia, Pennsylvania." The date beneath the inscription was 1792.

"It's a beautiful book," Aileen said as she carefully turned the pages. The family record section in the center of the Bible was filled with fine, spidery writing. The ink had faded, and many of the names written there were no longer legible.

"I just wish I could read it," Verna said wistfully. "Isaac reads from it sometimes, and that's a pure comfort, but it would be nice to be able to do it myself."

Aileen looked up from the Bible. "You can't read?"

"Shoot, ma'am, ain't many of us can around here."

After a moment's consideration, Aileen said slowly, "We may have to see what we can do about that."

She closed the Bible, and Verna refastened the latch. Then they went outside to unload more of the goods from the wagons. As they worked, Aileen chatted brightly, hoping to draw Verna out of her shell. She learned from the young woman that several of the settlers' children were suffering from the grippe.

Travis was finding Tommy Parks to be less friendly. The young man answered almost entirely in monosyllables when the marshal tried to question him about what had been happening since their arrival on Needham's ranch, and the young man did not volunteer any information. Travis, growing frustrated, realized that it would take a great deal of effort to establish any relationship with this distrustful, angry young man. When Aileen announced that she was ready to go on to some of the other cabins, the marshal was more than happy to leave.

At their next stop they found Orion McCarthy and Isaac Parks hard at work helping put up the soddy that would house a man, his tired-looking wife, and their multitude of children. Travis looked at the brood of youngsters and said in a low voice to Orion, "I think they're going to need a bigger soddy."

"Aye," Orion answered with a grin.

One of the children was coughing. Aileen gave the mother a small bottle of medicine and dosage instructions. The woman took it gratefully and said with downcast eyes, "We can't pay you, Doctor."

"I don't want any payment now," Aileen told her. "Perhaps later, when you've harvested your crop and have something extra, you might bring some vegetables to town."

"We sure will, ma'am," the father said solemnly. "Sure do appreciate you comin' out here to tend to us like this."

"It's my pleasure," Aileen assured him.

She and Travis continued on their rounds of the sod cabins. None of the children the doctor examined were seriously ill, but she did ease the symptoms of their minor ailments. She and the marshal were unable to cover the entire area of Needham's ranch, but now that Aileen knew the way—and the settlers knew her, which was just as important—she could return at another time. Late in the afternoon, she and Travis returned to the soddy where Orion had been working. The Scotsman mounted his big bay and joined them for the long ride back to town.

"What do you think, Orion?" Travis asked him as they rode. "Can these people make a go of it here?"

"If hard work and determination count for anything, they kin," Orion answered. "They've had so much hard luck, though, they'll not believe it till it happens."

Travis agreed. At each soddy they had visited throughout the long afternoon, he had sensed the settlers' strong feelings of impending trouble. It was as if they were simply waiting for something terrible to happen.

Dusk was falling when the three friends crossed the bridge over Mud Creek and walked the horses into Abilene. Orion said, "I hope Augie has had no trouble today. The lad's new at the bartending profession."

"I'm sure he did fine," Travis commented. Peering

74

through the shadows, he noticed a dark shape halfway down Texas Street. "Isn't that buckboard tied up in front of your office, Aileen?"

"Yes, it is," the doctor answered, a note of worry coloring her voice. She flicked the reins and urged her horse to a trot. "I hope whoever it is hasn't been waiting long."

Travis and Orion flanked her buggy as she hurried down Texas Street. When she drew the buggy to a stop, the man who was sitting on the seat of the parked buckboard stood up and turned to face her. Aileen recognized him as Bert Sprague, a man who had a small ranch east of town.

Sprague's ten-year-old daughter, Wilma, was lying in the back of the buckboard, covered with a blanket. The child was moaning softly.

"You've got to help me, Doc," Sprague pleaded anxiously. "My little girl's sick. You've got to help her."

"Of course, Mr. Sprague." Picking up her medical bag, Aileen quickly got down from the buggy. Travis had already dismounted and was tying up her horse to save her that much time. Aileen said, "Bring her on into the office, so that I can take a look at her."

Sprague stepped over into the bed of the wagon and bent to slide his arms under his daughter's slender form. Wilma moaned as he picked her up. Orion stepped directly from the saddle into the wagon bed and said to Sprague, "Let me take her, man. I'll hand her down t'ye."

The rancher nodded and, after gently transferring the girl to Orion's arms, hopped to the ground and stretched his open arms to take the child. Orion carefully handed Wilma to him. The two men had been as cautious and gentle as possible, yet the girl still sobbed with pain.

"I'm sorry I wasn't here when you came," Aileen said over her shoulder as she hurried up the walk to the office. She stepped up onto the porch. "I was out tending to some sick children belonging to those new settlers."

Bert Sprague stopped in his tracks at the bottom of the steps leading to the porch. "You've been out to Needham's place?" he asked harshly.

Aileen turned toward him, puzzled. "Why, yes. Come on, Mr. Sprague. Bring Wilma on into the house."

Sprague shook his head. "No. I'm not lettin' you touch my girl."

The doctor stared at him, stunned. Travis and Orion had heard his angry statement and were equally surprised. Aileen said, "What are you talking about, Mr. Sprague? She's obviously very sick. She needs my attention as soon as possible."

"Not after you've been out there tendin' to those Southern trash. Who knows what kind of pestilence you might be carryin' back with you?"

"Here now, there's no call to talk like that, Sprague," Travis admonished him.

The rancher turned toward him, clearly prepared to reply angrily, when Aileen broke in.

"Mr. Sprague, Wilma is sick!" she blazed furiously. "How dare you deny her medical treatment just because you have some stupid, bigoted idea about those settlers?"

"She's my girl," Sprague began defensively. "I got my rights—"

"The right to stand there and let her die?"

Wilma whimpered again as Aileen's sharp words lashed through the air.

"Them sodbusters don't belong here—"

"That has absolutely nothing to do with your daughter's condition!" Aileen snapped. "At least have the common decency to tell me what seems to be wrong with her."

"Well, she's been hurting in her belly, hurting something fierce to hear her tell it. Started up all of a sudden. At first we figured she just had a bellyache from something she ate, but it's not gettin' any better."

Aileen stepped from the porch and reached out to touch the girl. Sprague started to flinch, then forced himself to stand still while Aileen gently probed Wilma's stomach. Wilma screamed.

"Get her inside! Her appendix has burst, you fool!"

Sprague hesitated for a moment, gaping at Aileen. Then Travis said quietly, "I'd do what the doctor says, friend."

Sprague nodded abruptly. He hurried up the steps and disappeared into the building, following Aileen, with the other two men close behind him. Over her shoulder, she flung commands at Travis and Orion. "Get some water boiling on the stove, Orion. Luke, you come and help me."

The two men exchanged a glance. They had not expected to be drafted into helping with this crisis, but neither man would think of arguing with Aileen Bloom at a time like this. Travis had never seen her so angry. Yet once the seriousness of the situation was known and she was free to intervene, she was in complete control—cool and efficient and completely professional.

Yes, Luke Travis thought as he and Orion hurried into the office to follow her instructions, Abilene was lucky to have a doctor like Aileen Bloom.

And she was really pretty when she was angry.

Chapter Five

---◆---

SATURDAY AFTERNOON WAS THE BUSIEST DAY OF THE week in Abilene. Most of the townspeople as well as the ranchers and farmers from the surrounding area routinely did their shopping then. Wagons, buckboards, and saddle horses lined the streets, and the stores bustled with customers.

Cody Fisher was in the Alamo Saloon, spending an hour or so away from the marshal's office. The dimly lit, smoke-filled room was a carbon copy of many saloons across the West. A long wooden bar stood along the right wall, the shelves behind it lined with bottles and glasses. Tables and chairs, occupied by cowhands, were scattered around the rest of the room. Painted women mingled with the cowboys, some sitting on laps, others dancing to the tunes played on the tinkling piano.

On this sunny afternoon, Cody was not drinking.

He was enjoying a penny-ante poker game with a couple of cowboys and one of the house dealers, a man named Stoner. The gambler laughed as he raked in a pot.

"It's a good thing I'm in this game strictly for the practice, boys," he said. "Otherwise you'd be borrowing against your wages for the next five years."

"Luck doesn't sit on one man's shoulder for too long at a time," Cody said as he studied the dwindling stack of chips in front of him. "It's as changeable as a woman."

Stoner laughed again. "Luck's got nothing to do with it, Deputy. I'm talking about skill."

The Alamo's batwings swung open, and two men entered. Cody did a double take as they crossed the floor toward the bar; an alarm sounded in his mind.

The men, who wore work shirts, overalls, and shoes, were vaguely familiar, and after a moment's thought Cody was able to identify them. They had been on the wagon train that had come through Abilene earlier that week and were part of the group of settlers from Georgia.

The noise in the saloon dwindled once the other patrons realized who the two newcomers were. Looking straight ahead, the pair of settlers went to the bar, not meeting the glares of the saloon's customers. The two cowhands at Cody's table shifted uneasily in their chairs.

As Stoner looked at the settlers out of the corner of his eye, he muttered, "Uh-oh, hope there's no trouble."

"Why should there be?" Cody asked casually, yet he watched the men intently as they ordered drinks from the surly bartender.

One of the cowboys at the table spoke up. "Hell, Cody, you know why them boys aren't welcome in here. They're farmers."

"There have always been farmers around here," Cody replied impatiently.

The other cowpuncher shook his head. "Not like them. Those other sodbusters have been here awhile. They know where they're supposed to stay. They ain't plowin' up land that's always been open range."

"And they're not from Georgia, either, are they?" Cody snapped.

"That's part of it," the first cowboy said. "My daddy fought in the war on the Union side. I ain't got no use for Rebels."

Cody sighed but did not bother to reply. Luke Travis had been right when he had said that words would not change the way anybody felt.

The two settlers had gotten their drinks and were finishing them now. Cody was thankful that they were minding their own business and were causing no trouble. As the patrons in the saloon began to relax once more, the sounds of talking and laughter resumed and grew louder. Music tinkled from the player piano. Other than an exchange of some hard glances, there had been no trouble, and Cody hoped it would stay that way.

The deputy breathed a sigh of relief when the two farmers turned away from the bar and started for the door. Then a cowhand who was dancing with a painted woman swooped toward them, whirling the woman in his arms. She yelped as she banged into one of the settlers.

The settler stepped back and muttered, "Careful, cowboy." The collision had been a minor one, and no harm had been done. The farmer and his companion started to move past the cowpuncher and the painted lady in the spangled dress.

Abruptly the cowhand grabbed the farmer's overalls and yanked the man toward him. "What the hell did you say to me, sodbuster?" he demanded in a loud, angry voice.

The farmer shook loose from the grip. "I said for you to be careful, mister," he replied, his own face flushing with anger. "You should watch where you and that harlot are dancin'."

The young woman looked up at the cowboy and whined, "You gonna let him get away with insultin' me like that, Carl?"

"Damn right I'm not!" Carl sneered. He seized the farmer's overalls again. "Take that back and apologize to the lady!"

At the table, Stoner's eyes rolled up. "Oh, no!" he said.

Cody was already in motion, scraping his chair back and rising to his feet. "Hold—" he began, but he was too late.

The farmer's knobby fist lashed out and smashed into Carl's unshaven jaw.

The young woman screamed as the cowboy staggered from the blow, but he quickly caught his balance and lunged at the settler. Both men began throwing punches. Then the second farmer jumped into the fracas, bear-hugging Carl from behind while the other man pounded fists into his belly. Another cowboy scooped up a beer bottle from a table and launched it at the head of the second farmer.

"Hold it!" Cody yelled once more.

The words had no effect. The two cowpunchers who

had been playing poker with Cody and Stoner leaped up and hurried to help their friends. Within moments, the struggling men battling in front of the bar were joined by all the other cowhands who had been drinking in the saloon. Outnumbered and overwhelmed, the two farmers went down in a welter of flying fists and boots.

Cody ran to the bar and yelled at the bartender, "Give me the shotgun!"

The bartender backed away, shaking his head. "I ain't goin' to let the place get shot up over some damn sodbusters!" he answered angrily. "Let 'em beat those farmers down into the ground, Deputy!"

Enraged, Cody cursed, and in a flash he drew his Colt, training it on the bartender. Then, fixing the man with a fierce scowl, he placed his other hand on the bar and vaulted over it. As his boots hit the plank flooring behind it, he reached down to pluck a sawed-off shotgun from the shelf where it was usually kept. Still glaring at the bartender, Cody holstered his pistol and pointed the shotgun's muzzle at the ceiling.

He touched off one of the barrels, and the blast was a deafening roar in the close confines of the saloon. Plaster rained down on the fighting men as the load of buckshot blew a hole in the ceiling above them. Stunned, the combatants froze as Cody trained the shotgun on them.

"Stop it right now!" Cody demanded sharply. "Next man who throws a punch is going to be dodging buckshot. Now back off."

Slowly, the cluster of cowboys battering the two farmers backed away. The settlers huddled on the floor, their faces bruised and bloody but rage still apparent in their truculent expressions.

Still pointing the shotgun at the cowboys, Cody said, "There'll be no more fighting in here. Carl, you started this ruckus. I say it's fair you pay for the hole in the ceiling."

"The hell I will!" Carl roared. "That sodbuster threw the first punch!"

"You pushed him to it," Cody replied coldly. "I was sitting right over there, remember? I saw the whole thing, and it looked to me like you were going to keep pushing until this man pushed back."

"I ain't payin' nothin'!" the cowboy insisted.

"All right," Cody said with a nod. "If you feel that way about it, you can march right over to the jail and take your chances with Marshal Travis. He'll probably charge you with assault or disturbing the peace and keep you in a cell to cool your heels for a while. My way, you're just out a little money."

Carl took a deep breath, let it out between clenched teeth, and then reached into his pocket. He pulled out a coin and tossed it to the bartender. "That's all I got on me," he growled. "I'll have to pay you the rest later."

The bartender nodded. "See that you do."

Cody looked at the two farmers, who were still sprawled on the floor. "You men get out of here," he said.

"We just came in here for a drink," one of the settlers snapped. "We got a right to do that."

"You do," Cody agreed, "but now it's time to move on."

Grudgingly, the farmers struggled to their feet and stumbled to the doorway, casting belligerent glances over their shoulders at the saloon patrons as they pushed through the batwings.

Cody sighed and handed the shotgun back to the bartender. "Sorry about the hole in the ceiling," he said. "But it looked like those two farmers were going to get stomped to death if I didn't do something."

"No great loss," the bartender muttered.

Cody stepped out from behind the bar. The pleasant game of poker had been ruined, and he decided to go to the marshal's office and see if Travis had anything for him to do. As the cowboys in the saloon gradually returned to their tables, picking up their drinks and cards and pulling the saloon girls onto their laps, Cody stalked toward the door.

The batwings burst open before he reached them. A man wearing a store clerk's apron ran into the saloon, yelling, "Somebody help! They're tearing the place down!"

Cody recognized the man as a clerk from Karatofsky's Great Western Store, which fronted Texas Street around the corner from the Alamo. From somewhere outside he heard yelling and crashing. Catching the clerk's arm, he snapped, "What is it? What the devil's happening?"

The man pointed a quivering finger. "It's a riot!" he exclaimed. "Around the corner in the store!"

The commotion was growing louder. Cody shoved the man aside and ran out of the Alamo, drawing his gun as he went.

The deputy raced down the boardwalk to the intersection of Texas and Cedar streets and careened around the corner. As he spotted the mass of struggling figures that spilled from the double doors of Karatofsky's Store and into the street, he slowed to a walk. A cloud of dust had already been stirred up and hung over the combatants.

Cody was not surprised when he saw that there were almost as many farmers as cowboys, though the cowpunchers seemed to be getting the better of the battle. Judging from the crashing and banging that came from inside the mercantile, the fracas was boiling in there, too.

Cody glanced down Texas Street and saw Luke Travis running down the boardwalk toward the riot, gripping his Winchester. When he reached Cody, Travis stopped and asked angrily, "What the devil . . . ?"

Cody smiled in spite of himself. "At least they're not trying to shoot each other," he said. "Maybe they won't do too much damage with fists."

Exasperated, Travis glanced at his deputy. "I heard a shotgun blast a few minutes ago and was about to check on it when this ruckus broke out. You know anything about that?"

"It was me," Cody admitted. "I broke up a fight in the Alamo between a bunch of cowboys and two of those Georgia sodbusters. The odds were just too uneven." He stepped aside as a cowboy with a battered nose reeled down the boardwalk. "You think we should make this bunch behave themselves, Marshal?"

Travis sighed. At least two dozen men were slugging each other in the street, and no one knew how many more were battling inside the store. Women and children had scurried out of the way and were now standing at a safe distance across Texas Street, gawking at the melee. One of the store windows was broken; the shattered glass crunched under the booted feet of the combatants. As he stood watching, Travis heard another particularly loud crash inside Kara-tofsky's.

"We'd better restore some law and order here," Travis said grimly. He pointed the Winchester toward the sky and squeezed the trigger. Levering shells into the chamber, Travis fired three more shots as fast as he could.

The rolling thunder of the shots froze the struggling men in their tracks. Farmer and cowboy alike turned surprised faces toward the two lawmen on the board-walk.

In the silence that followed on the street, Travis could hear the racket coming from inside the store. "Put a stop to that ruckus in there, Cody," he ordered. Then he turned to the men in the street and shouted, "This fight's over! I'll haul the whole lot of you to jail if I have to!"

Cody stepped into the store, his Colt drawn and ready in case somebody decided to take a shot at him. He stopped just inside the doorway and glanced around the shop. He could not believe the chaos he saw.

Piles of merchandise had been knocked over and lay in tatters and smashed heaps in the aisles. A pickle barrel had been overturned, creating a sour-smelling lake next to the big main counter. Several groups of men were still throwing punches at each other.

The deputy blasted a shot into the ceiling and then dropped the muzzle of his gun to cover the brawling men, who froze at the sound of the shot. "Outside, all of you!" Cody snapped.

He herded the men into the street, where they joined their companions. Travis had ordered the two groups to separate, and now the cowboys stood to the right of the store's porch, the farmers to the left. From his position in the center of the porch, Travis glared at all of them.

"What in blue blazes happened here?" he demanded as Cody stepped up beside him. Scanning the crowd, Travis spotted Tommy Parks. "Get up here, Tommy!" he ordered.

Tommy came forward with his face set in sullen lines. "It wasn't our fault, Marshal," he muttered. "It was those other fellows who started it."

"He's lyin', Marshal!" a cowboy called out. "We was just mindin' our own business when them sodbusters jumped on us."

"You weren't doing anything to provoke them?" Travis asked sarcastically.

The cowboy shuffled his booted feet in the dust of the street. "Well, we mighta been funnin' 'em a mite. . . ."

Travis nodded. "I figured as much. So somebody took exception to what you said and threw a punch. That was all it took to start this brawl." Travis looked at Tommy Parks again and asked, "Where's your pa? Did he come in with the rest of you?"

Before Tommy could answer, Isaac Parks's deep voice called from a distance, "I'm right here, Marshal."

Travis and Cody looked down the boardwalk to see Isaac emerging from the doorway of an apothecary's shop down the block. Behind him, peering around the door, were several of the settlers' women and children.

"I figured I'd best get the women and the youngsters out of harm's way when that fighting started," Isaac said as he reached Travis and Cody. He waved a gnarled hand at the angry men standing in the street. "I was afraid someone would get hurt."

Travis rested the barrel of the Winchester against his shoulder. "Did the whole bunch of you come into town today?" he asked.

"We needed supplies," Isaac answered. "We thought it might be safer to ride in together."

Travis took a deep breath. "Somebody's going to have to pay for the damages here, Mr. Parks. I think the only fair thing to do is split it down the middle."

"But . . . but we don't have any money, Marshal."

"You go inside and talk to Mr. Karatofsky," Travis instructed him. He glanced over his shoulder and saw the storekeeper peeking cautiously through the broken front window. "You work it out with him. He's a reasonable man." Turning to the group of cowhands, Travis continued, "You cowboys get up here and dig in your pockets. I want your whiskey and tobacco money and whatever else you've got on you. Toss it in Deputy Fisher's hat and then be on your way."

Cody grinned as he swept off his black, flat-crowned hat and turned it over to collect the money. "I feel a little like a banker," he joked as the coins clinked against each other in the headgear. The cowboys muttered curses as they parted with their free cash and headed for their horses.

"Cody, keep an eye on things here," Travis said. "Mr. Parks, you and your people get the supplies you need and load them on your wagons. Then you come down to my office. I want to talk to you for a few minutes."

"All right, Marshal," Isaac agreed. He seemed shaken by the violence he had witnessed.

As the crowd dispersed, Travis turned and strode

toward his office. Cody remained on the boardwalk, collecting money from the remaining cowboys and watching for more trouble. The settlers dusted themselves off and went into the mercantile to gather up their supplies. As Tommy passed by him, Cody said, "You might help Mr. Karatofsky straighten up his store. Might make the marshal feel a little less angry at you folks."

Tommy grunted in agreement.

Saturday afternoon in Abilene, Cody thought, had never been quite like this.

During his trek down Texas Street, Luke Travis barely contained his fury. Once he arrived at the jail, he stormed into the office, slammed the door, hurled himself into his desk chair, and raged silently at the walls for several minutes. When the door opened a few moments later, he had regained his composure. He glanced up sharply, expecting to see Isaac Parks and ready to deliver the lecture he had just formulated. Instead, Aileen Bloom stepped into the office. Travis pushed his chair back and got to his feet.

Aileen shook her head and waved him into his chair. "Don't bother with formalities, Luke," she said. "Just tell me what happened. It sounded as if the Civil War was being waged all over again."

Travis grimaced. "That's about what it amounted to. A bunch of cowboys and those settlers from Needham's place got into a brawl at Karatofsky's."

Aileen moved to one of the chairs in front of the desk and sat down. "Was anyone hurt badly?" she asked.

"I don't think so," Travis replied, shaking his head. "Cody and I broke it up pretty quickly. I saw plenty of cuts, bruises, and bloody noses, but I don't think there was anything worse than that."

"I saw the settlers earlier when they arrived in town. It looked as if all of them came along, even though they didn't bring all of the wagons."

"That's what Isaac Parks told me," Travis said. "They thought it would be safer that way, but it backfired on them."

"What are you going to do about this situation, Luke? It's liable to get dangerous." Aileen's deep brown eyes clearly expressed her worry and concern.

"It already is," Travis replied.

At that moment the office door opened, and a nervous Isaac Parks stepped tentatively into the office. When he saw Aileen, he tugged off his hat and nodded to her. "We're about ready to pull out, Marshal," he said. "You wanted to talk to me?"

"That's right, Mr. Parks."

"Isaac."

Travis shrugged. "All right, Isaac. You know as well as I do that the cowboys don't want you and your people here. It's only going to stir them up when they see a whole bunch of you coming into town."

"Are you saying we shouldn't come to Abilene, Marshal?"

"No, I'm not saying that at all—"

"Because we've got a right to come and buy supplies. You know that, Marshal."

With a frustrated nod, Travis said, "I know. But I'm just telling you to be reasonable. You can't go around trying to start trouble."

Isaac's features had lost their diffident expression, and an angry frown spread across his lean face. "Those cowboys started that fight," he said. "If you'd heard some of the things they said to our women, you'd know that." He glanced at Aileen, and his expression softened. "Pardon me, ma'am."

"That's all right, Mr. Parks," Aileen replied. "I can well imagine what some of those cowboys had to say."

Travis pushed back his chair and stood up. "I'm sorry about that, but it doesn't change the facts. I don't want to see more than four or five of you in Abilene at one time, you understand?"

Isaac stared at him for a long moment, then said coldly, "I understand." He turned and walked out of the office, his back stiff and his eyes straight ahead.

Travis stood looking at the closed door for a long moment, then uttered a heartfelt curse. He looked at' Aileen and shook his head, "I didn't handle that very well, did I?"

"Maybe not. But you said what you thought needed to be said. There's no point in the settlers doing something that might provoke more trouble."

"No, but they have every right to come into town, just as Parks said." Travis sat down heavily. "They've got me in the middle. All I want is peace and quiet here in town."

Aileen leaned forward. "You've been a lawman long enough to know that you can't please everyone, Luke. All you can do is enforce the law as fairly as possible."

Suddenly the tense frown left his handsome face, and his features lit up in a warm grin. "And all you can do as a doctor is what your knowledge of medicine tells you is possible. But that doesn't mean you quit worrying about your patients, does it?"

Aileen shook her head. "You're right, Luke," she admitted with a chuckle. "Doctors still worry, even when we know there's nothing else we can do. What about marshals?"

"We worry," Travis said simply.

During supper that night, Tommy Parks quietly nursed a swollen jaw and ate little. Isaac cheerfully tried to make conversation, but the stony silences he received in response forced him to abandon the effort. As he finished his supper, he was certain that there were quite a few silent suppers in the other soddies on Needham's ranch. Everyone was brooding over what had happened in Abilene earlier in the day.

Once Verna had served the stew, she said nothing. She watched Tommy with soulful brown eyes and looked as if she wanted to do something to soothe his seething emotions but could not figure out just what.

Finally, when the meal was over, Isaac leaned back in his chair and said, "Tomorrow's the Sabbath, so we'll rest. But first thing Monday morning I want to finish that plowing we started this morning, Tommy."

"Sure, Pa," Tommy replied thickly. He pushed his bowl away and reached for his cup of coffee. He seemed able to sip the hot liquid without hurting his jaw too much.

Isaac frowned and looked up. "You hear something?" he asked. The sounds of shooting and yelling were faint at first, barely audible in the sod cabin.

Tommy hesitated, listening intently. "Guns!" he said abruptly. "Sounds like riders comin', Pa!"

Both men were on their feet instantly, Tommy hurrying to the corner for Isaac's ancient rifle while his father rushed to the doorway, pushing back the canvas curtain that covered the opening.

"Wait a minute, Pa!" Tommy called after him, but it was too late. Isaac was already outside.

The yelling was louder now, clearly audible over the cracking of pistols. Tommy ducked through the doorway, the sound of hoofbeats filling his ears, and spotted his father standing several feet away. In the moonlight he could see Isaac staring at the field where earlier in the day they had started turning the earth in preparation for planting their crop.

Men on horseback were storming through that field now, waving guns in the air and firing them, whooping exuberantly as their horses trampled through the plowed earth. It was too dark to see the faces of any of the men, but they were obviously cowboys.

Tommy stood beside Isaac, tightly clutching the rifle in his hands. The young man's breath came faster, and he abruptly brought the rifle's stock to his shoulder.

Isaac lashed out, grabbing the barrel of the rifle and forcing it back toward the ground. "No!" he snapped. "You'll just get us killed, boy!"

The leader of the group of cowboys suddenly twisted in his saddle, brought his pistol down, and aimed it at the two men standing in front of the soddy. Tommy, from over his father's shoulder, saw what was about to happen. Uttering an inarticulate cry, he grabbed Isaac and dove to the ground.

Flame darted from the muzzle of the cowboy's gun. Once, twice, three times it blasted, the slugs whining over the heads of Isaac and Tommy to thud into the walls of the soddy. Then the cowboy let out another yell, savagely spurred his horse, and galloped away from the would-be farm. The other raiders followed him, still firing into the air.

Tommy rolled over and leaped to his feet. "Verna! Verna, you all right, gal?" he called anxiously as he ran to the doorway of the soddy.

The young woman appeared, framed in the lantern light, and nodded. "I'm fine, Tommy," she quavered. "Just scared, is all."

Tommy took her into his arms and held her tightly for a long moment.

Isaac struggled to his feet and stared into the darkness where the cowboys had disappeared. No real harm had been done—this time. But Isaac knew what this meant, and he murmured, "My God, my God. It's just starting. . . ."

Chapter Six

———◆———

Isaac Parks's gloomy prediction proved to be accurate. Over the next week, trouble visited the D Slash N nearly every night, sometimes in several places. The local cowhands were taking great delight in tormenting the farmers, stampeding cattle through the newly plowed and planted fields, fouling ponds and creeks, and generally torturing the settlers from Georgia.

A few of the more foolhardy farmers tried unsuccessfully to fight back. Those who dared to shoot at the marauders had to dive back into their soddies in a hail of bullets. It was only blind luck that no one was killed or seriously wounded.

Not much could be done about these raiders who galloped onto the farms in the black night, wreaked havoc, and disappeared into the protection of darkness. Reports of the attacks reached Luke Travis daily, and he seethed in frustration, powerless to stop the harassment. Although he was convinced that Brice

Dixon was involved in most of the attacks, he had no concrete evidence to prove it.

As if the problems on Needham's ranch were not enough, Travis also had trouble in town. The fights in the Alamo and Karatofsky's Great Western Store had only been the opening rounds in the battle between the farmers and the cowhands. Travis and Cody were kept busy breaking up saloon fights. The city coffers increased with the fines that Travis imposed on brawlers in an attempt to discourage fighting, but even that measure did not stop the fights. Short of swearing in a dozen special deputies and making the whole town off limits to cowhands and settlers alike, there was nothing more Travis could do.

Isaac Parks was just as upset as Travis. He had made the arrangements with Needham and led people to Kansas to make a fresh start in their lives. Now, despite all his efforts, the dream of a new life was crumbling. But Isaac knew only one way to deal with disappointment and frustration: He had to keep trying, to keep working the land he had chosen for himself and his family.

One bright morning, he was plodding along behind his mule in front of the soddy, steering the plow and making fresh furrows in the field that had been chopped up the night before by wild cowboys, when he looked up and noticed a man on horseback and someone in a buggy approaching from the direction of Abilene.

Isaac stopped working and wiped his forehead. As they drew nearer, his keen eyes made out the sober suit of the Methodist minister, Judah Fisher, and the heavy black habit of the nun, Sister Laurel.

At least these two were not coming to cause trouble,

Isaac thought. He glanced around the field and noticed that Tommy and Verna were nowhere in sight. They had probably gone to one of the fields behind the soddy, on the other side of the rise. Isaac was relieved; Tommy was so hostile to anyone from Abilene that his father was glad he was not present to see these visitors.

Judah lifted a hand in greeting as he reined in. Beside him, Sister Laurel pulled the buggy horse to a stop. Judah said, "Hello, Mr. Parks. How are you?"

"Tolerable, I suppose," Isaac answered. He nodded to the nun. "Hello, Sister."

"Mr. Parks," Sister Laurel replied. "The Reverend Fisher and I decided to ride out and see how you and your friends are doing."

"Thank you, both of you. We appreciate the concern. Why don't you come into the cabin? There's some cool spring water there."

"We didn't mean to take you away from your work," Judah began.

A tired grin split Isaac's lined face. "Pastor, I'd welcome any excuse to stop this plowing for a while. That sun gets to a man after a few hours."

"Indeed it does," Judah agreed. "We'd be glad to join you for a drink of water."

Isaac turned the mule around, and the little group rode to the soddy. Several days earlier, Tommy had placed two poles in the ground a few feet in front of the doorway and stretched some canvas from them to the soddy wall, creating an awning of sorts. The shade beneath the canvas felt cool and welcome to Isaac as he picked up the water bucket and the dipper that sat by the door.

"Come on in," he said. "It's more comfortable inside."

The two visitors joined him in the soddy, and Isaac found cups for them and dipped water from the bucket. As the three of them sat down at the rough table placed in the center of the neatly arranged, clean cabin, Judah said, "I want to invite you and your friends to attend services at my church anytime you feel like it, Mr. Parks. Everyone is always welcome."

"Well, thank you, Pastor," Isaac replied. "I've done quite a bit of reading in the Good Book myself. Three or four times all the way through it, in fact. I usually do a little preaching on the Sabbath."

"Oh," Judah said. "I wouldn't want to interfere with your services. . . ."

Isaac shook his head. "They're not really services like in a real church. We'd be honored to visit sometime and hear you preach."

Judah grinned. "We'll all be glad to see you."

Sister Laurel had been unusually quiet. Now she leaned forward and said, "Mr. Parks, I want to talk to you about another matter. Dr. Bloom mentioned to me that most of your people are unable to read and write."

"That's true," Isaac admitted. "My ma taught me to read when I was a youngster, and I've done my best to teach Tommy, but most of these folks never had any time for schooling. I don't imagine any of the children around here can read."

"Then you'll be glad to know that we've made arrangements for the children to attend school in Abilene," Sister Laurel said. "I have quite a bit of experience with children, and I can tell you how important an education is to their welfare."

Isaac looked down at his hands and frowned. After a long moment, he looked at her and said, "That's true, Sister, but I don't know how these families will feel about sending their kids away from their work. Many families depend on these youngsters to work in the fields. We need all the help we can get while these farms are getting started."

"I'm well aware of the practice of using children to help out in the fields, Mr. Parks," Sister Laurel answered. "But a child who cannot read and write will never be able to do anything in the world." Her stern voice softened somewhat. "It took some convincing to get the town council to see things our way, but that's something the reverend and I are good at. Surely you can persuade your friends to allow their children to attend school."

Isaac leaned back in his chair and thoughtfully rubbed his jaw. After a moment, he said, "You're right, Sister. Learning's the best way—maybe the only way—out of the troubles those youngsters will be facing as they grow up." He suddenly smiled across the table at his two visitors. "I'm sure I speak for all of us when I say we'd be glad to have them go to your school."

"It's your school, too, Mr. Parks," Judah pointed out. "You and your friends are part of our community now."

Isaac laughed humorlessly. "I just wish the rest of the folks around here felt like that, Pastor. I expect you've heard about the troubles we've been having out here."

Judah nodded, his light blue eyes darkening angrily. "I certainly have," he said, "and I think it's awful that you're being treated so rudely. The ranchers are going to have to learn that there's enough room here for everybody."

"For some folks, there's never enough room," Isaac said sadly.

Neither Judah nor Sister Laurel could argue with that. Both of them had seen ample evidence that some people could never be satisfied, no matter how much money or land or power they possessed. Usually it was the little folks, like Isaac Parks and his friends, who got stepped on and pushed aside in the never-ending quest for more of everything.

But a start had been made today, a beginning of cooperation between the town and the settlers. Sending the children to school was the first step.

All three people sitting around the table hoped it would work out better than things had so far.

Dr. Aileen Bloom was sitting in her office a few days later, working on her patients' files, when the front door of the house opened. Putting her pen down, she stood up and walked to the doorway that led into the front room, expecting to see either a patient or Luke Travis waiting there. It was late in the afternoon, and the marshal frequently dropped by at the end of the day to take her to dinner.

Instead, a short, slender man with thinning brown hair and a sour expression stood there. He wore a brown suit and a string tie and stood with his arms folded, impatiently tapping one foot.

"Why, hello, Mr. Simpson," Aileen said as she stepped into the room. She was surprised to see Abilene's schoolmaster. "What can I do for you?"

Thurman Simpson did not take off his hat or even touch the brim in greeting. He seemed to be too angry to worry about being polite. That was not uncommon, Aileen thought. Simpson was usually angry about something.

"You can send those horrible children back where they came from," the teacher snapped.

"What children are you referring to, Mr. Simpson?" Aileen asked in mock puzzlement. She believed she knew the answer already.

"Those illiterate little monsters from Georgia. I'm told it was your idea that they attend school here in town."

"There's no other place where they can be taught, Mr. Simpson. I just mentioned to Reverend Fisher and Sister Laurel that none of them can read or write."

"And those two do-gooders ran right to the town council to make life more difficult for me," Simpson sniffed.

Aileen felt her face flush with anger at Simpson's obnoxious attitude. "I believe it is your job to teach," she said, keeping her voice level and calm. "Then the children won't *be* illiterate."

Simpson waved a thin hand. "Those children won't learn, Doctor. I don't believe they're even capable of learning. All they're suited for is pulling a plow, like the beasts of burden they are."

Aileen took a deep breath, making a great effort to control her temper. Rather than lashing out at Simpson, she asked sweetly, "Have they been causing problems in class?"

"Of course they have," Simpson snapped. "They're children, aren't they? And they're accustomed to living an undisciplined existence. They have no re-spect for authority at all."

Aileen knew only too well that authority meant a great deal to Thurman Simpson. The man thrived on the power he exerted over his students and had clashed with many people over his roughshod teach-ing methods. Cody Fisher had threatened to take a hickory switch to Simpson if the teacher did not stop whipping the children so frequently. But many of the parents supported Simpson and approved of his harsh methods. He was also the only teacher the town council had been able to keep in the job for more than a few months.

"Not only are they as wild as Indians," Simpson went on, "but the school is packed to bursting now. It was bad enough when all of those . . . those orphans were allowed to attend the school. Now, each day more of those urchins come in from Mr. Needham's ranch. I simply cannot continue to teach under these conditions, Doctor."

"Then what do you suggest we do about the situa-tion, Mr. Simpson?" Aileen asked tightly.

Simpson sneered. "Tell those Southern children that they are no longer welcome. I realize nothing can be done about the orphans without that nun upsetting the entire town, but at least we can get rid of those poor white trash."

Appalled by his words, Aileen stared at him. She slowly drew a deep breath and shook her head. "There's a town council meeting in three days, Mr. Simpson," she finally told him. "All I can say is that you should attend and express your opinions to the entire council."

"I plan to do just that," Simpson declared. Without

another word, he turned and stalked from the doctor's office.

Aileen watched him go. As the door slammed behind him, she looked down at her hands and saw that her fingers were trembling with the anger she still felt. She would be certain that she attended the council meeting, too, to make sure that someone spoke up in opposition to the venom that Simpson planned to spew.

Suddenly, a smile curved Aileen's lips. An idea had occurred to her, and the more she considered it, the more sense it made to her.

Let Thurman Simpson express his complaints. She would have a little surprise waiting for the schoolmaster.

At seven o'clock on Thursday evening, the town council met in Abilene's courthouse. Every member was in attendence. The seven men and one woman—Dr. Aileen Bloom—sat at a long table in the front of the room. Aileen was a new member on the council, and her mere presence was quite a coup. At first the seven businessmen who made up the council were leery about a woman serving with them. But Aileen's personality and medical skills had impressed the town's citizens, and in the last election she had overwhelmingly defeated her opponent and been elected to the council.

Several rows of chairs had been set up facing the table for spectators and people who wished to bring complaints before the council. Luke Travis sat easily in one of the chairs, his right booted foot resting lightly on his left knee, his hat on the floor beside his chair. He regularly attended the council meetings in case the officials had any questions for him about law and order in Abilene.

Thurman Simpson was also there, sitting at the opposite end of the marshal's row. A few other citizens were present when the meeting began, but nothing about the low-key proceedings warned of the fireworks that would soon explode.

The council first disposed of several routine matters. Then the mayor turned to the audience and said, "All right, is there any other business to be brought to our attention?"

Since Aileen had alerted the other council members that the teacher would be there to speak to them, no one was surprised when Thurman Simpson popped up from his chair. "I have something to say, Mr. Mayor," Simpson declared.

"All right, Thurman," the mayor replied. "Go right ahead."

"I want to lodge a complaint about the excessive work load that is being placed on me," Simpson said. "Due to the meddling of certain elements in this town"—he glared pointedly at Aileen as he spoke —"the children of those farmers from Georgia have been allowed, even encouraged, to attend school here in Abilene. And I am expected to teach these little ruffians, most of whom have had no previous education at all!"

The mayor stared silently at Simpson for a moment. Then he leaned forward and said mildly, "Well, Thurman, I figured that teaching kids is how you earn that salary we pay you. Isn't that the idea of a school?"

"Indeed," Simpson snapped back. "But now there

are simply too many students for one teacher to instruct properly."

"What do you think we should do about that?"

Simpson's lip curled in a sneer. "The solution seems obvious to me. We simply do not allow children who live outside the town limits to attend our school."

Another council member spoke up. "Kids from the outlying farms and ranches have always come into town to go to school, Mr. Simpson, ever since we built that school. It doesn't seem fair to make them stop now."

"Well, perhaps all of the children should not be excluded," Simpson said. "I would be satisfied if only the newest arrivals were told to leave."

Aileen could contain herself no longer. "You want to single out the children of those families from Georgia."

Simpson stared coldly at her. "That would satisfy me, yes. Such a move would reduce the number of students to a level that could be managed by one teacher."

Surprisingly, Aileen smiled as she turned to address her fellow council members. "As Mr. Simpson stated earlier, the solution to the problem is obvious, gentlemen. If there are too many students for one teacher, all we have to do is hire another teacher."

Murmurs of surprise rose from council members and audience alike. A wide grin stretched across Luke Travis's face. Aileen had shared her plan with him earlier, and he had thought it was a good one. She had also told the mayor, who was now nodding.

Simpson's eyes widened in shock. "A-another

teacher?" he stammered. "I don't need another teacher, I just need fewer students."

"It seems to me that it works out the same either way," Aileen replied.

"Except that it costs us more," one of the councilmen said.

The mayor leaned forward. He had taken some persuading during Aileen's private meeting with him, but he had come around to her way of thinking. Now he said, "I think Dr. Bloom's got a point. Abilene's a growing town. We're going to keep on growing, and we're going to need another teacher sooner or later. We might as well get somebody in here now and get started."

"No!" Simpson exclaimed. "I don't want—"

"You don't want any help, Mr. Simpson?" Aileen cut in. "I thought you said you were overworked."

Travis swallowed the laugh that threatened to burst from his lips. Thurman Simpson was beginning to look positively sick.

Aileen smiled sweetly as she looked at Simpson. She knew why he was opposed to hiring another teacher, and so did everyone else on the council. Simpson had enjoyed a free hand in the schoolhouse for a long time, and he did not want anyone to come in and challenge his authority.

The discussion among the council members was lively for a few minutes, but with Aileen and the mayor speaking in support of the proposal, the others were soon convinced. The salary for a new teacher was the only sticking point, and Aileen was able to point to areas in the budget where the money could be found. When the council members at last voted on hiring a new teacher, the proposal passed unanimously.

Thurman Simpson sat pale and shaking, helpless to do a thing to stop the council's action.

"All right," the mayor said. "That's settled. You'll have to get along by yourself for a while until we can get another teacher, Thurman, but I'm sure you'll manage."

Simpson swallowed and nodded.

Aileen chose that moment to reveal the rest of her plan. "It shouldn't be too long, Mr. Simpson," she said. "I took the liberty of contacting an agency back East that supplies teachers for frontier schools." She reached into the pocket of her skirt and withdrew a piece of paper. "I received a telegram from them this afternoon. They've located a recent graduate of one of the teachers' colleges who is willing to accept the position in Abilene. Her name is Leslie Gibson, and according to this telegram, she's available to travel here as soon as the council votes to hire her."

"And I believe that vote was just taken," added the mayor.

This news caused another small hubbub, but it died down when Simpson sniffed, "Very well. I see now just how much weight my opinion carries around here. You might have at least consulted me before hiring some flighty girl who's probably not much older than my students." He put his hat on. "She won't be much help, I'll wager, but I suppose I can't expect much more." With that, he stalked out of the court-house.

After Simpson left, the large room was silent for a

moment. Then the mayor said softly, "You know, I kind of feel sorry for any teacher whose first job is working with Thurman Simpson."

Aileen silently agreed. She hoped she was not letting Leslie Gibson in for more trouble than the woman had bargained for.

Chapter Seven

JUDAH FISHER HAD KNOWN HARD TIMES IN HIS LIFE, BUT he had never known poverty, not with a father who had been a respected lawyer and judge. As he visited the community of farmers on Doyle Needham's land, he saw firsthand what it was like to be dirt poor, and he was appalled by the ugliness.

The sight of children so pitifully thin that their limbs were like sticks was painful to Judah. The youngsters' clothing was threadbare and ill-fitting. Parents who were probably no more than twenty-five years old easily looked twice that age. These people had known only hardship and a continual struggle to survive, and the heartrending evidence of the effort tugged at Judah.

The reverend made frequent trips to the D Slash N, sometimes on his own, sometimes accompanying Dr. Aileen Bloom on her rounds of the farms. Luke

Travis, concerned for Aileen's safety because of the continuing trouble with the area's cowhands, had asked him to ride with her, and Judah had been glad to comply. He admired Dr. Bloom and enjoyed her company.

He was alone, however, the day he rode up to the Parks farm and found the soddy deserted. Judah called out repeatedly, but there was no answer from the earthen cabin. He was about to turn his horse around and ride on to another dwelling when he heard bellowed curses coming from the far side of the rise behind the Parks soddy.

Judah walked his mount to the top of the slope and looked around. In the middle of the gradually sloping field, he saw Tommy and Verna struggling valiantly to move a large rock. Tommy, his shoulder against the rock, was shoving as hard as he could, but the boulder was embedded in the earth and refused to move. He uttered more curses as he heaved against the rock. Verna worked beside him, helping as best she could, and it was she who glanced up and saw Judah Fisher sitting on his horse.

"Tommy!" she said sharply. "Hush!"

"What?" Tommy drew back from the boulder, clearly surprised that she would speak that way to him.

Verna nodded toward Judah, who walked his horse slowly forward as Tommy looked around and saw him.

Tommy looked defiant rather than embarrassed as Judah rode up. He nodded curtly and said, "Pastor."

"Hello, Tommy," Judah replied. He touched the brim of his hat. "Hello, ma'am."

"What do you want out here?" Tommy asked. He pulled a cloth from his pocket and wiped his face.

"I came to talk to your father, but I didn't find him at the cabin," Judah explained.

"He's over to the Ellison place," Tommy said. "You could ride over there if you want to talk to him."

Judah shook his head. "Oh, no, it was nothing urgent. I just wanted to see how all of you were getting along. I'll talk to him later." He gestured at the large rock. "It appears that you're having some trouble."

Tommy glared at the boulder. "This ol' rock's been here right along, and I'm getting tired of plowing around it."

Judah dismounted. "Perhaps I can lend a hand," he said.

Tommy eyed Judah's lean form. "Don't guess you'd be much help, Pastor," he said bluntly.

"Oh, you'd be surprised," Judah replied with a grin. "I've been told I'm rather wiry."

Tommy grimaced disdainfully and put his shoulder against the rock. "Suit yourself," he grunted.

Judah slipped off his dark coat and held it out to Verna. "If you'd be so kind as to hold this, my dear," he said.

"Sure, Pastor," Verna said, taking the coat from him. She looked almost as dubious as Tommy about Judah's ability to help move the boulder.

Judah stepped beside Tommy and placed his shoulder against the boulder. He found grips for his hands and then set his feet in the dirt. "I'm ready when you are," he said.

"All right," Tommy said. "On the count of three. One, two, three . . . !"

Both men straightened their legs, throwing their weight and strength against the boulder. For a moment it seemed as firm and unyielding as before. But then the rock lurched. The movement was small—only a fraction of an inch—but it encouraged the two men. They paused to gasp some fresh air, then lunged against the boulder once more.

With a slight sucking sound, the big rock came free of the dirt where it had rested for so long. It began to roll, slowly at first, then gaining momentum and picking up speed.

"Stay with it!" Tommy yelled. He kept his weight against the boulder and worked his legs to make sure the rock did not come to a stop. Luckily, the boulder had been weathered and rounded by the elements so that it rolled fairly easily.

As they neared the edge of the field, the two men gave the boulder a last vigorous shove, sending it rolling off the field into a clump of smaller rocks. Tommy and Judah stood watching as it came to a halt. Their arms hung limply at their sides, and they were breathing heavily.

"Well . . . we did it!" Judah said triumphantly.

"Damn right we did!" Tommy agreed. He abruptly clamped a hand over his mouth. "Uh, sorry, Pastor. Didn't mean to cuss in front of you."

Judah clapped him on the shoulder. "Don't worry about it, Tommy. That rock was so stubborn that it deserved a little cussing."

"Come on back to the soddy with us. Don't know about you, but I could use a drink of cool water."

"Sounds good," Judah agreed.

Verna handed his coat to him. Instead of putting it

on, he draped it over one arm, and the three of them walked over the rise to the soddy. When they were in front of the cabin, Tommy passed around the water bucket and the dipper. Judah found the water cool and good, and it went a long way toward restoring the energy he had burned up in helping to move the boulder.

"That's good," he said as he handed the bucket to Tommy. "You're lucky to have such a good stream close by."

Tommy nodded. "It's only a couple of hundred yards down to the creek. I been thinkin' that when Pa and me get the time, it might be a good idea to dig a ditch over there so we could get water easier."

"That's interesting," Judah agreed. "It might make this land even more productive."

At last Verna spoke. "Tommy has lots of good ideas about farming," she said proudly. "We'll do just fine here if folks will let us alone."

"Yes," Judah agreed, his voice becoming more solemn. "I'm so relieved that the trouble is beginning to cease. I've been praying that there won't be any more."

"No offense, Pastor, but prayin' isn't going to stop those fellows. Sooner or later, it's going to come down to shooting."

"I hope not, Tommy," Judah said fervently. "There has to be a way to solve the problems without violence."

"Only other way is to run." Bitterness tinged Tommy's voice. "The way we ran out of Georgia. Some of us wanted to stay and fight there, but Pa talked us out of it. Said it'd be better to come out here and start over, rather than getting more folks killed. The war had already killed enough," he said.

"Too many," Judah said. "Any deaths are too many."

Tommy smiled, but there was no humor in the expression. "That's the preacher in you talking. Some folks just need killing, like those carpetbaggers who came in and took over our farm and killed my ma when they did it. They got our place and dozens of others around us. It was all legal, they said. Wasn't a thing we could do about it." The young man grimaced. "The folks who didn't want to leave, well, they got burned out or shot. Supposed to be the government, but they're nothin' but a bunch of thieves and murderers."

"I . . . I know it was hard back where you came from."

"It sure was, Pastor. It sure was." Tommy looked up suddenly. "Look there, Verna! That stubborn ol' cow's got loose again!"

Verna and Judah followed his pointing finger and saw a milk cow ambling across one of the fields, the piece of rope that had served as an inadequate tether trailing behind her. Verna said, "I'll go get her," but Tommy waved her back with a hand.

"I'll round her up," he said. "Take a stick to her and teach her some sense, that's what I ought to do." He loped off across the field after the cow.

Judah watched him for a moment, then turned to Verna. "Your brother is a rather angry young man," he said.

"He's not my brother," Verna replied. "He's pretty mad about everything that's happened, though."

Judah frowned. "I was under the impression that you and Tommy were brother and sister."

Verna shook her head. "Nope. My name's Verna Sills. My folks were friends of Isaac's. They . . . they were killed a while back, just before we were supposed to join the wagon train with the others."

When she hesitated, Judah asked softly, "Was it the carpetbaggers?"

The girl shook her head. "No. My pa didn't like them, but he wasn't a fighting man. A wagon turned over, and both my ma and pa were under it. I . . . I guess that's why I was so scared when that wagon ran away with me when we were on our way here."

Judah had heard about the runaway wagon from Cody. Now knowing how Verna's parents had died, he understood her terror very well.

"Anyway, after the accident, Isaac took me in and said he'd bring me out here with the others," she went on. "Him and Tommy are the only family I've got now."

Judah nodded. He studied Verna's face as she watched Tommy rounding up the straying cow, and he saw something in her eyes that he had missed when he thought they were brother and sister. Admiration and affection were in Verna's gaze, but something deeper was lighting her brown eyes. She was in love with the young man.

With this realization, Judah's mind began to churn. Verna was an attractive young woman, and Tommy a handsome young man. They lived in the same cabin. It was only natural that an attraction would develop between them. Judah started to frown. This was a decidedly improper arrangement.

On the other hand, Isaac Parks lived here, too, and Judah had seen enough of the man to know that he was decent and honorable. Isaac would see to it that nothing happened until the two young people were married.

And Judah was suddenly sure that sooner or later Tommy and Verna would be married. It had to be. He smiled. Perhaps they would let him perform the ceremony in the church. That would be something to look forward to.

Tommy was grinning as he led the cow back. He tied it securely to the stake, then returned to the soddy. The hostility within him seemed to have subsided. "Thanks for helpin' me with that rock, Pastor," he said. "It'd still be there if you hadn't come along."

"Please, call me Judah. And I was glad to be of help. That is part of my calling, after all."

Tommy extended his hand. "Next time you ride out here, we won't put you to work," he promised. "You will be coming this way again, won't you?"

Judah nodded, gripping Tommy's hand. "I'll be back," he said.

Cody Fisher ambled across Railroad Street and headed for the Abilene depot of the Kansas Pacific Railroad. The large, red-brick building sat beside the tracks, which ran at an angle through the heart of town. One of Abilene's busiest areas, the depot bustled, especially when a train was expected, and the two-fifteen was scheduled to arrive from the east within a quarter hour.

Cody walked into the station building and cut through the waiting room, which was filled with families, drummers, gamblers, and even a soiled dove or two. A few of them were here to greet passengers who would disembark in Abilene, but most were waiting to board the in-coming train and journey westward.

As he strolled onto the long, covered platform next to the tracks, Cody spotted the slight form and pinched features of Thurman Simpson, who was standing a few feet away. Simpson had his hands jammed in his pockets and was tapping one foot impatiently.

Cody, pushing his hat back on his head, stepped over to the schoolteacher. "Howdy, Thurman," he said with a broad smile. "You come to meet the train, too?"

Simpson glanced at him through slitted eyes. "Is that an official question, Deputy?" he snapped.

"No," Cody replied. "I just figured you might've heard that the new schoolmarm was due to come in on the next train, like I did."

Simpson frowned. "Who told you?"

"Dr. Bloom."

"I might have known," Simpson muttered. "That woman seems to mind everyone's business but her own."

Cody stopped grinning. "This is her business, since she's responsible for getting a new teacher to help you."

"Yes. Don't think I've forgotten that."

"You think she'll be young and pretty?"

"I don't know, and I don't care," Simpson sniffed. "All I know is that she is inexperienced, which means she'll be of little or no help to me."

"I think I should brush up on my spelling," Cody

118

went on jokingly. "Maybe Miss Gibson will agree to some private tutoring."

Simpson, glaring disdainfully at Cody, said nothing.

Cody shrugged and moved over to one of the posts that supported the roof over the platform. Leaning against it lazily, he looked down the tracks to the east.

Thurman Simpson is a first-class idiot, Cody thought. He had figured out also why the teacher was waiting for the train: Simpson wanted to be certain Miss Gibson knew right away who was in charge in Abilene. He wanted the poor little gal under his thumb from the moment she climbed off the train. The more he could run roughshod over her, the more he would lessen his own work load.

Cody, however, had come simply to welcome Leslie Gibson, or so he told himself. He was performing his duty as a public official and a representative of the town. The chance that she might be young and attractive had nothing to do with it.

The mournful wail of a train whistle jarred Cody from his thoughts. Straightening and peering down the tracks, he squinted beyond the sprawling stockyards at a pinpoint moving across the prairie. Within moments, the tiny form enlarged to the looming shape of the approaching train.

With the brakes screeching as it slowed to a stop, the locomotive rolled into the station in a billowing cloud of steam. The engineer expertly stopped the train so that the passenger cars were aligned with the platform. The conductor, hopping from the caboose to the platform, ran along the cars, shouting, "Aaaabilene! Abilene town!"

As the travelers began to emerge from the cars and step onto the platform, Cody scrutinized each one, looking for a woman resembling a schoolteacher coming to her first job. They came in all ages, shapes, and sizes. Several middle-aged ladies traveling with their husbands disembarked, as well as a few pigtailed girls belonging to families of immigrants. But no one who might fit the description appeared. It seemed as if Leslie Gibson's arrival had been delayed for some reason.

Cody frowned and glanced at Thurman Simpson. To his surprise, the schoolmaster wore a worried grimace. For all his bluster, Simpson had probably been looking forward to having some help. He was clearly disappointed.

So was Cody. "Shoot," he muttered as he watched the final passenger climb from the train. This last person was a tall, broad-shouldered, bearded man who carried himself with an easy grace that belied his burly physique. Cody paid little attention to him, but the man spotted the deputy's badge pinned to Cody's shirt and started toward him.

Cody, seeing the man coming, noted the well-cared-for suit, the derby hat, and the catlike way the big man moved. The deputy's well-honed instincts told him that this stranger was an experienced, dangerous fighter, and he began to wonder uneasily what such a man was doing in Abilene.

"Excuse me, Deputy," the man said in a deep, rasping voice. Simpson was scanning the passengers, watching for a young woman he might have overlooked. The stranger went on, "Could you tell me where the schoolhouse is?"

A few feet away, Thurman Simpson's head snapped around. Cody frowned. Suddenly a bizarre possibility occurred to him, and he began to grin. Nodding toward Simpson, he said to the stranger, "This gentleman here is the teacher. I'm sure he'll be glad to show you the way to the school."

The newcomer's heavy features brightened in a pleasant smile. He turned to Simpson and extended a hamlike hand. "Mr. Simpson? I'm glad to meet you, sir. My name is Leslie Gibson."

Simpson gawked at the big man in undisguised shock while Cody tried not to laugh out loud. For several seconds the schoolteacher visibly struggled to master his distress. At last raising a limp hand, he weakly returned Leslie Gibson's handshake.

Cody thrust out his hand to Leslie Gibson and said, "I'm Cody Fisher, Mr. Gibson. We're glad to meet you, aren't we, Thurman? We came down here to do just that, didn't we?"

Simpson nodded shakily and made a noise in his throat that could have been taken for an affirmative.

Glancing past Gibson's bulky form, Cody noticed that Orion McCarthy was standing next to a freight car, supervising the unloading of some supplies for his tavern. Rather than focusing his attention on the crew handling the cases, however, the tavern keeper was staring at the burly man shaking hands with Thurman Simpson. Cody watched in amazement as recognition lit Orion's eyes.

Abruptly, Orion turned away from the freight car and hurried to the newcomer. With an excited expression on his face, he said heartily, "Ye be Slugger Gibson, the heavyweight from New York!"

Startled, Gibson winced, sighed, and then nodded. "That's right," he admitted. "I no longer go by the name Slugger, though."

Orion grabbed his hand and pumped it enthusiastically. "'Tis a pleasure t'meet ye, lad! I saw ye take on Kid Randisi years ago."

"That was a long time ago," Gibson said sheepishly. "I'm a teacher now, not a prizefighter."

Cody could not believe his ears. With each exchange, the situation was getting better. Simpson looked devastated. He had expected some flighty young girl, and instead he had gotten this big bruiser.

"I realized that a life in the ring doesn't leave you with much when you have to retire," Leslie Gibson was saying. "I appreciate this chance to get started in teaching, Mr. Simpson. I'm sure I'll learn a lot once I start working with you."

Barely containing the laughter that threatened to burst from him, Cody glanced at Orion, who was grinning broadly. The Scotsman clearly understood what was going on, and the humor of the situation was not lost on him. Cody had not relished a moment such as this in a long time.

Simpson had still not said a word. Leslie Gibson peered at him and with a puzzled expression asked, "Is anything wrong, sir? There's no problem about my job here, is there?"

Simpson shook his head and finally found his tongue. "No . . . no problem at all," he said hoarsely. "I . . . I have to be going now. Deputy Fisher can show you the school." He turned and almost ran toward the depot.

"That'll be fine, sir," Gibson called after him. "I'll be there first thing in the morning!" As Simpson disappeared into the station building, Gibson turned back to Cody and Orion. "Did I say something to bother Mr. Simpson? He seemed awfully upset about something."

Cody had all he could do to contain himself. He clapped the big man on the shoulder. "Oh, I guess you just weren't quite what he was expecting."

"Well, I hope he's not disappointed."

"I dinna know about Mr. Simpson," Orion said warmly, "but I kin tell ye tha' none o' the rest o' us be disappointed."

"That's right," Cody chuckled. "There'll be time later to show you the schoolhouse, Mr. Gibson. Right now, let's all go have a drink. Orion here has the best whiskey in town."

"That sounds good," Gibson replied. "Let me tend to my baggage. Is there a good boardinghouse in town where I can have it sent?"

"Aye. Come wi' me and we'll see t'having it delivered."

A few moments later the three men were strolling down Texas Street's boardwalk toward Orion's Tavern. As they made their way, Cody pointed out the local landmarks: the Alamo Saloon and the Bull's Head, the marshal's office, the Sunrise Café, the Grand Palace Hotel, Dr. Bloom's office, and finally Orion's itself. Once they had entered the cool, shadowy interior of the tavern, Cody and Gibson went to one of the tables while Orion moved behind the bar to collect a bottle and some glasses. The three men sat down.

Orion splashed whiskey into the glasses and then lifted one to propose a toast. "T' Slugger Gibson," he said, "the best damn heavyweight these old eyes ha' ever seen!"

The three of them drank, and Leslie Gibson sighed appreciatively. "That is good," he said. "I don't take a drink very often. Have to set a good example for the children, you know."

Cody leaned back in his chair. "If you don't mind my asking, how did a fighter end up teaching school, Mr. Gibson?"

"Call me Leslie, please." Despite the gravelly nature of the big man's voice, he was surprisingly gentle and soft-spoken. "I had to get out of the fight game after a while, so I decided to try what I'd always dreamed of doing. I went back to school and learned how to be a teacher." He shook his head. "Boxing aroused a brutal side of me that I would rather not see."

"Aye, I recall how ye handed the Italian his head tha' night," Orion said. "'Twas a real terror ye were, me friend."

The big man, looking down at his hands resting on the table, appeared to be embarrassed. "I try to control that now. It's not good for children to see violence or even know about it, so I would be grateful if you would keep that part of my past a secret."

"Sure," Cody agreed readily. "It sounds to me like you really care about kids."

"I love them," Gibson said simply. "Always have. In fact, the only thing that really sets me off now is somebody being cruel to a child."

Cody and Orion exchanged a meaningful glance. Cody knew that Orion was thinking about the harsh way Simpson treated his students. The same thoughts were in Cody's mind. The working relationship between Leslie Gibson and Thurman Simpson was going to be interesting to watch.

Chapter Eight

———◆———

THE DAY THAT JUDAH FISHER HAD HELPED TOMMY
Parks move the boulder marked the beginning of a
growing friendship between them. During the next
week the minister paid several visits to the Parks
farm, sometimes helping with chores, at other times
simply sitting and talking with Tommy, Isaac, and
Verna. At first they would not talk about the problems
that had forced them to leave Georgia, especially
Isaac. But as Judah drew them out, he learned in great
detail what hardships the poor white farmers had
endured under the Reconstruction government. After
hearing of their plight and considering it, Judah
decided that Isaac and his friends had been justified in
leaving Georgia. They had followed a course of action
with which he was sympathetic. He did not believe in
answering violence with violence except as a last
resort. On a more practical level, the settlers would

most likely have been killed if they had continued to oppose the government.

Late one afternoon, after spending the better part of the day visiting several other soddies, Judah stopped at the Parks farm. The settlers had not yet responded to his invitation to attend services at the Methodist church, so he had been bringing the Gospel to them, ministering to their spiritual needs just as Aileen tended to their medical needs.

As Judah dismounted, a wary Tommy Parks came through the soddy doorway. The tense young man carried a rifle and behaved as if he expected trouble. When he saw that the visitor was Judah, he lowered the rifle and relaxed.

"Has there been more trouble, Tommy?" Judah asked anxiously.

"Just more of the same," Tommy answered. "Not here, but over at the Morrisons'. Last night some men drove a herd of cows through their cornfield and ruined it."

"I thought the cowboys around here were getting tired of that sort of thing. The harassment was beginning to stop, wasn't it?"

"For a while. It's back now." Tommy's voice was grim. "Now that our crops are starting to take hold, I guess those bastards think they can do more damage. Sorry, Judah."

Judah shook his head, more than willing to overlook the young man's profanity under the circumstances. "I'm sorry to hear about the Morrisons' trouble," he said.

Tommy nodded. "Yep. My pa's over there now, tryin' to help them figure out what to do next."

"Can't Mr. Needham help in some way? Can't he stop these raids from taking place?"

"He's done what he can," Tommy said with a shrug. "He put up some bob wire, but those punchers just cut it and trample it down. I guess Needham's got enough troubles without taking on ours."

"He was quick enough to bring you here," Judah pointed out. "He should bear some responsibility for your well-being."

Tommy patted the stock of the rifle. "'Fraid we're going to have to be responsible for ourselves, Judah."

The canvas flap covering the doorway of the soddy was pushed aside, and Verna poked her head through the opening. "Hello, Pastor," she said with a smile. "Tommy wanted me to stay inside until he saw who was ridin' up, but I reckon it's safe to come out now."

Judah returned her smile. "I imagine it is."

"Why don't you stay to supper?" Verna asked as she came out of the cabin. "We've got plenty."

Judah doubted that very seriously. He knew the settlers had been making do with short rations ever since they had arrived. He shook his head and said, "Thank you for the invitation, Verna, but I've already promised to have dinner with Sister Laurel tonight. We have some matters to discuss concerning the children."

Surely the Lord would forgive such a small bending of the truth, Judah thought. Although they had made no specific plans to eat together, he and Sister Laurel did usually dine at the same time, and not a day went by when they did not have to talk about some of the orphans. As with any group of children, they got into plenty of mischief, especially the adolescents.

"Maybe some other time then," Verna said.

Judah nodded. "I'd like that."

While Judah and Verna had been chatting, Tommy was peering across the field over Judah's shoulder. Suddenly the young man stiffened and, with a glance at Judah, said, "Dagnab it, there goes that cow again! Wish I knew what was on the other side of that hill behind the house that she's so all-fired determined to get."

Judah followed Tommy's gaze and saw that the milk cow was loose once more, as it often seemed to be. Even as they spoke, the animal, which was halfway across the field in front of the soddy, was gamboling briskly around the earthen cabin and up the hillside from which the soddy was dug. The three friends watched as the roving beast disappeared over the ridge in back of the soddy. Judah pulled his reins to turn his horse. "I'll go round her up," he volunteered. "I've never been mistaken for a cowboy, but I think I can manage to herd one cow back."

Verna stepped in front of his horse. "No need to bother, Pastor," she said quickly. "I'll chase the critter back here."

"It wouldn't be any trouble—" Judah began.

Shaking her head, Verna interrupted him. "You just stay put and talk to Tommy. Maybe you two men can figure out how you can keep those raids from startin' up every night again."

As she started after the straying cow, Judah and Tommy exchanged sympathetic glances and shrugged. Judah slowly dismounted and tied his horse to one of the poles that supported the canvas awning over the soddy's door.

"Come on inside," Tommy said. "There's coffee on the stove, even if you can't stay for supper."

"Now that sounds good," Judah agreed. He could smell the rich aroma, and it reminded him of how tired he really was. He stepped into the soddy.

Once over the ridge, Verna spotted the cow tramping through a newly sprouted field of corn. Eager to stop the big animal's destructive romp, she scurried across the field, carefully moving between the rows to limit the damage she herself did. When she reached the animal, she examined the tether rope and saw that the cow had chewed through it. Verna shook her head. The cow was placid and cooperative in every respect but this one.

So engrossed was she in her task that she did not see or hear the horseman riding up from the west. When she suddenly noticed a long shadow appear next to her, she dropped the tether abruptly, spun around, and lifted a hand to shield her eyes from the glare of the setting sun. She saw a rider reining in a few yards away, but the brilliant red orb was behind him, silhouetting him so that she could not make out his features.

"Well, howdy, darlin'," a smooth voice said. "What's a sweet-looking gal like you doin' out here by herself?"

Nervously, Verna brushed a strand of chestnut hair from her face. "I . . . I was just after that cow over there," she said, pointing a shaking hand at the animal.

The man turned his head and looked. The sun illuminated his profile, and Verna could see that he was a young man. Her eyes began to adjust to the glare, and she began to notice some details. He was slender and probably not too tall, although that was hard to determine while he sat in the saddle, and he wore well-cared-for range clothes.

"Hell, that's just a broken-down old milk cow," he said contemptuously. "Not hardly worth calling beef."

"I still have to get her."

"I'll round her up for you," the young man said. He started to swing down from the saddle. "In a little while, that is."

As the man's booted feet touched the plowed earth, Verna stepped back involuntarily. She knew he was a cowboy and realized he might be one of the punchers who were causing so many problems for the settlers. From his clothes, she guessed he was probably well-to-do. To a man like him, she would be just a pretty little sodbuster gal, to be trifled with as he pleased.

"I've got to go," she said nervously as she took a few more faltering steps backward. "My . . . my family's waitin' for me to bring that cow back."

"Oh, they won't mind if you're a few minutes late." The cowboy dropped the reins of his horse. He walked slowly but confidently toward Verna. "You're about the prettiest thing I've seen on this hardscrabble spread," he went on. "You're one of that bunch that's sharecropping on Needham's land, aren't you?"

"Wh-what if I am?"

The man shrugged. There was a broad grin on his lean, handsome features. "There's no call to be scared of me. I don't have anything against sodbusters, especially when they look like you. Why don't you come here and give me a kiss?"

Verna struggled to control the fear that threatened to overwhelm her. In a voice that shook more than she wanted, she said, "You just leave me alone, mister. I don't want to make you mad, but I've got a beau already."

"One of those Southern trash?" the cowboy sneered. "I've heard about you Southern gals. Hell, you were probably rutting with the boys by the time you were twelve, weren't you?"

Anger flared within Verna, blunting the fear she felt. "You've got no call—"

The man had slowly diminished the distance between them, and now he suddenly lunged and grabbed her. His hand closed over the soft flesh of her upper arm, bare in the sleeveless dress she wore. "Shut up!" he blazed as he yanked her close to him. "I know all about you white trash! I know all the women are whores—"

He broke off to bring his lips down hard on hers. Verna tried to yell, but his urgent mouth stifled her. He started to wrap his other arm around her and tried to press his body against hers.

Terror gave Verna unexpected strength. She tore her mouth away from his, jerked her arm from his grip, and twisted her body away from his brutal embrace. Her hands came up and shoved hard against his chest, staggering him. She seized the opportunity to whirl around and run back toward the ridge and the safety of the soddy beyond.

Cursing furiously, the cowboy started after her, but within a few feet, he was lurching in the soft, plowed earth. A horseman's boots were not made for running in such terrain, and he turned and hurried back to his horse.

Verna was sprinting through the field, her skirts lifted, her thighs flashing as she ran. Vaguely, she heard the profanity that her assailant flung after her. She could still taste the hot foulness of his mouth. He had been drinking.

Hearing hoofbeats, she threw a frantic glance over her shoulder and saw his angry leer as he rode after her. Panic forced her to run more desperately, but as she did so she realized despairingly that, while she might be able to reach the ridge before he caught up with her, she would never make it all the way to the soddy. She opened her mouth.

"Tommmmyyy!" she screamed.

Tommy and Judah had been futilely hashing out the settlers' problems when Verna's frightened cry shattered their peaceful conversation. Tommy's head snapped up, and he gasped, "Verna!" He lunged toward the doorway, not thinking in his haste to scoop up the rifle.

Judah was right behind him. He had recognized the pure terror in Verna's voice and knew she had to be in danger to sound like that.

As the two men ran out of the soddy, they turned toward the ridge behind it. At that moment Verna appeared, running as hard as she could. As she topped the ridge, she seemed to stumble and suddenly fall, rolling over and over down the gentle slope.

The two men watched helplessly as a rider lurched over the top of the ridge, obviously chasing Verna.

An inarticulate cry burst from Tommy's lips. He snatched up an ax that was leaning against the soddy wall, and holding the sharp-edged tool tightly in both hands, he started running toward Verna.

Judah hurried behind Tommy, trying not to let the

hotheaded young man get too far ahead of him. As he raced after the younger Parks, Judah thought there was something familiar about the rider.

Verna's tumbling body came to a stop at the bottom of the rise, about fifty yards from the soddy. Slowly, she pushed herself up onto her hands and knees, shaken by her fall but apparently not hurt too badly.

The horseman, expertly working his mount down the slope, reined to a halt just as Tommy reached Verna's side. Standing over her, Tommy faced the horseman and raised the ax threateningly.

Judah was only a few steps behind him. Twilight shadows crept over the scene, but there was still enough light for Judah to recognize the man on horseback. The rider was Brice Dixon, the son of rancher Hunter Dixon and, according to Cody, probably the instigator of the raid on the wagon train east of Abilene. Judah knew Brice to be an arrogant young man, the kind to seize any opportunity to make trouble. The kind who would probably enjoy gunning down a sodbuster—

As he saw Brice's hand moving toward his holstered gun, Judah flung himself at Tommy, his hands grasping the ax handle and wrenching it from the young man's grip as his shoulder rammed into him, knocking him a few steps to the side.

"Dammit!" Tommy howled. "What—"

Judah turned and flung the ax, spinning it away across the field. He whirled around and shouted to Brice Dixon, "We're unarmed!"

"Judah, what are you doing?" Tommy demanded.

Ignoring Tommy, Judah stared warily at Brice, whose hand rested on the butt of the still-holstered gun. Slowly, Brice moved his hand away from the pistol, and a grin stole across his face. "Smart move, Preacher," he said. "You've just saved this trash sodbuster's life—for now."

"I figured you couldn't claim self-defense if we were unarmed, Dixon," Judah said coldly. "Now, why were you chasing this young lady?"

Verna got to her feet and threw herself into Tommy's arms. She buried her face against his chest and sobbed, "He tried . . . tried to . . . molest me!"

"That's a damned lie!" Brice snapped. "When I rode up, this gal was trying to catch some old milk cow, and all I did was offer to help her. I was just trying to be friendly."

"He got off his horse and grabbed me!" Verna twisted in Tommy's embrace to glare at Brice. Tommy was quivering with anger as he held her.

"I think we know what really happened," Judah said. "You'd better be moving along, Brice."

Brice swung a leg around the saddle horn and sneered arrogantly, "I'm used to riding where I please, Preacher."

"This is my land," Tommy told him. "I want you off it."

"Last I heard, this was Needham's range. You sodbusters run him off or something?"

"Never mind about Needham," Judah said. "Just leave, Brice, or I'll swear out a complaint against you."

Brice laughed harshly. "Based on what? The word of some sodbuster whore?"

Tommy made a noise low in his throat and started to step forward, but Verna gripped him more tightly. "Don't do it, Tommy," she pleaded. "He's got a gun."

"And he'd love an excuse to use it," Judah added.

He held his breath, not sure what Tommy was going to do.

"All right," Tommy said. "We'll go back to the soddy." Keeping Verna in the circle of his arms, he turned and started toward the cabin. Judah stared at Brice Dixon until the young cowboy chuckled, shrugged his shoulders, and turned his horse around. Putting the spurs to the animal, Brice galloped off.

With a sigh of relief, the minister turned and hurried after Tommy and Verna. When he reached the two young people, Tommy glared at him. "Why'd you do that, Judah?" he demanded. "It wasn't any of your business."

"I didn't want to see Brice Dixon gun you down," Judah replied. "If you had come at him with that ax, he would have done it. He knows how to use that gun, and he enjoys doing it, too."

"Well, he's not the only one who can tote a gun."

Judah grimaced. That was exactly the response he did not want to hear from Tommy Parks.

When the Methodist pastor reached the outskirts of Abilene, night had fallen. Worry over the incident at the Parkses' gnawed at him during the long ride, so rather than going directly home he decided to stop at the marshal's office. He was relieved when he saw a light burning in the building as he rode down Texas Street.

When Judah entered, he found Travis in the office and Cody sweeping out the empty cellblock. The deputy looked up at his brother with a sheepish grin and said, "Some job for a gunslingin' lawman, isn't it, Judah?"

"Somebody's got to do it," Travis commented. "Howdy, Judah. Something we can do for you?"

"I'm not sure," Judah replied. "But I'm afraid there's going to be trouble."

Quickly, he outlined what had happened at the Parks farm. Cody put his broom aside, his face hardening, as he heard what Brice Dixon had tried to do to Verna.

When Judah had finished his story, Travis nodded grimly. "I think you're right to worry, Judah," he said. "Brice would like nothing better than to have an excuse to draw on Tommy Parks."

"I told Tommy to stay out of town for a while," Judah told the two lawmen. "But I'm not sure he'll do it."

The marshal turned to Cody. "Keep your eyes open for Tommy Parks," he instructed. "He's hotheaded enough to strap on a six-gun and find himself in more trouble than he can handle."

After the brawls in the Alamo and Karatofsky's Great Western Store, the farmers had taken Travis's advice and come into town in smaller groups. They knew it would be foolish to come alone, so they usually traveled in groups of five or six when they needed supplies.

On the Saturday following the encounter with Brice Dixon, Isaac, Tommy, and Verna broke that pattern, riding in by themselves. Tommy walked his horse down Texas Street, his face an expressionless mask. Driving the wagon beside Tommy, Isaac was clearly nervous, darting worried glances at each saloon they passed. Verna sat huddled next to Isaac on the wagon seat, staring at her hands, not daring to raise her eyes.

Tommy wore a shell belt around his waist, an old holster dangling from it. Stuffed into the worn leather sheath was a gun—an old Colt with walnut grips worn smooth with age and use. The butt plate was nicked from the times when it had doubled as a makeshift hammer. Clearly, the Colt had seen better days, but it was a gun, and it meant something when it was worn on a man's hip.

Once the trio was stopped in front of Karatofsky's Store, Tommy swung from the saddle and tied up both his mount and the team pulling the wagon. Isaac stepped onto the boardwalk in front of the mercantile and helped Verna climb down.

After he and Verna had walked to the store's front door, Isaac turned to Tommy and said, "Come on, son. Let's quickly get those things we need so we can get back and do a few more chores this afternoon."

"You mean so we can turn tail and run back home as fast as we can," Tommy replied. He leaned against the railing at the edge of the boardwalk. "You go ahead, Pa. I think I'll stay out here."

"Now, Tommy, it was your idea to come to town today," Isaac pointed out. "The least you can do is help Verna and me."

"You can handle the supplies, Pa." Tommy's voice was cold and hard.

"Tommy . . ." Verna began.

"Sorry, Verna." He shook his head, cutting her off. "I don't feel like shopping today after all."

Verna and Isaac exchanged tense, worried looks. They both knew why Tommy had insisted on coming to Abilene today and why he did not want to go into the store. He was waiting to see Brice Dixon.

Even if Brice was not in town today, there were plenty of cowboys around. Once they had seen Tommy, some of them were bound to ride for Hunter Dixon's Rafter D ranch to carry the word back to Brice. If the showdown did not come today, it would still be soon, and all three of the settlers from Georgia knew it.

Isaac sighed. "Come on, Verna," he said. "We might as well get what we came for." With his arm around the young woman's shoulders, Isaac opened the door and went on into the store.

Diagonally across the intersection from Kara-tofsky's Store was the Old Fruit Saloon. It was doing the usual brisk Saturday-afternoon business. Trying to cram a week's worth of pleasure into half a day and one night, cowboys from all the surrounding spreads packed the establishment. Tommy noticed several punchers glance furtively at him, then hurry to the Old Fruit and disappear inside.

He was not surprised when, a few minutes later, a familiar figure pushed through the batwings of the saloon and strolled onto the boardwalk.

Brice Dixon lounged against the saloon's wall for a moment, casually glancing up and down Texas Street. Then his gaze fell on Tommy and stayed there. Even from across the street, the young farmer saw the eager grin on Brice's face.

That act fools no one, Tommy thought. As he straightened from his negligent pose, he watched Brice step into the street and begin to walk slowly across the intersection toward Karatofsky's.

Tommy stood on the boardwalk, letting Brice come to him. His heart began to pound harder as the cowboy approached, fear mixing with the anger that had driven him to come here today wearing a gun. But his anger and hatred of Brice Dixon still had the upper hand. As far as Tommy was concerned, the cowboy's attack on Verna had changed a campaign of harassment into a personal battle.

At the corner, Brice stepped onto the boardwalk about twenty feet from Tommy. He halted there, still grinning, and said, "Well, howdy, sodbuster. Lose any more milk cows lately?"

"No, but we had a hell of a time roundin' up the one we've got, thanks to you," Tommy replied coolly.

"Now, that wasn't my fault," Brice insisted. "I offered to help the gal get that beast back. She turned me down."

Tommy heard the door open behind him, but he did not dare take his eyes off Brice Dixon. He heard Verna gasp. Then Isaac said sternly, "I want you to come in here, son."

"I don't think so, Pa."

Brice laughed and said, "There's the little lady now, sodbuster. Why don't you ask her again what happened? Of course, she may forget to mention anything about the way she kissed me."

"That's a lie!" Verna cried.

"Get back inside, Verna!" Isaac snapped.

Brice's gaze bore into Tommy. "She's a right nice kisser, farm boy. But you'd know that. You and the old man both have probably been plowing that ground for a long time now."

Tommy's fingers trembled. He swallowed, all too aware of the crowd that was gathering. The bystanders stood out of the line of fire, but they were close enough to hear Brice's filthy comments. "I want you to leave us alone, Dixon. Us and all the other folks out at Needham's."

"Or what, sodbuster?" Brice asked mockingly.

"I'll have to make you leave us alone."

Brice laughed again. He pointed at the ancient Colt on Tommy's hip. "With that? Why, I've never seen such a sorry-looking excuse for a gunfighter before. How about showing me how you handle that gun, boy?"

Tommy took a deep breath. The challenge was out in the open now. There was nothing left to do but answer it.

Before he could even begin his draw, he saw a flicker of movement from Brice. With an awful certainty, Tommy realized he could not beat Brice to the draw. He was going to die here and now—

"Go ahead, Brice," a voice boomed through the afternoon air. "You go right ahead and finish what you're doing. Then you'll have to turn around and face me."

Brice froze, his fingers still a couple of inches from the butt of his gun. Slowly, he turned his head until he could see the lean figure behind him. A cold smile was chiseled on Cody Fisher's face as he waited, thumbs hooked casually in his gun belt.

Noticing Cody, Tommy called, "This isn't any of your business, Deputy."

"Folks shooting each other in Abilene's streets is exactly my business," Cody replied. "Brice is going to kill you, Tommy, and then I'm going to kill him. Right, Brice?"

The young cowhand hesitated, still motionless. Abruptly he shook his head. "Not today," Brice said harshly. Sneering at Tommy, he went on, "You're not worth wasting a bullet." He turned and strode across the intersection, pushing a couple of his cronies roughly aside as he entered the Old Fruit Saloon.

The blood was hammering in Tommy's head as Cody walked up to him. Although he knew how close he had come to dying, the young farmer was angry at Cody for interfering. "You didn't have to—" he began.

"Yes, I did," Cody cut in. "It's my job to keep fools from getting themselves killed. Why don't you take that gun off, Tommy? It's not going to do anybody any good."

"We'll see." Tommy heard the quick footsteps behind him and turned to take Verna in his arms. The woman was pale with fright. He patted her on the back and tried to reassure her.

Isaac said, "Thank you, Deputy. You saved my son's life. But I'm afraid that young man won't forget this."

Cody nodded in agreement. "Too many folks saw what happened. Brice backed down. They know it, and he knows it. That's just going to make him angrier at you people. Maybe some good will come of it, though."

"I don't see how," Isaac replied gloomily.

"Look at it this way," Cody said. "Brice Dixon has a score to settle with me, now."

Chapter Nine

———◆———

Aileen Bloom sat in an overstuffed armchair in Mrs. Chester Symington's parlor, sipping tea and nibbling on a small, tasteless sandwich. Around her the ladies of Abilene's leading social committee twittered and gossiped.

During the first few minutes of the gathering, Aileen had listened politely and tried to participate, but she had quickly realized how little she had in common with these women. She spent her days extracting bullets, setting broken bones, and tending to sick children, not worrying about the latest fashions from the East.

However, Mrs. Symington and the other members of the social committee had asked her to join, and Aileen had decided it would be wise to accept the invitation. The husbands of these ladies were the most powerful men in Abilene. Between the influence she could exert through this committee and her own position on the town council, Aileen believed she could make a difference in the way the town was run. This was the 1870s, after all, not the Dark Ages, and it was time Abilene grew up.

Now, as she sat in the stuffy parlor, Aileen wondered if she had made a mistake. This was the first committee meeting she had attended, and if they were all like this, she knew she could not justify taking this precious time away from the other, more worthwhile things she could be doing.

The grating sound of Mrs. Symington's voice jostled the doctor from her thoughts. "Don't you think so, dear?" she asked Aileen with a smile on her heavily powdered face.

Aileen blinked. "I'm sorry, Mrs. Symington," she said as she focused her attention on the woman. "I'm afraid my mind was wandering."

"I was just saying that the spring dance, which will be held the Saturday after next, is going to be wonderful this year," Mrs. Symington repeated a little stiffly.

"I'm sure it will be," Aileen agreed. Actually, she had given little thought to the annual celebration. She knew that the committee usually invited the whole town and that the ranchers and farmers from the surrounding area also participated.

Mrs. Symington turned away, sniffing. Aileen thought she might have made a bad impression on the lady, but she refused to worry too much about it.

A heavy knock on the front door surprised the ladies and silenced all conversation. With a frown, Mrs. Symington looked toward the door and said, "Now who could that be? Chester knows we're having our meeting tonight; he won't be back until he's sure it's over."

Aileen's lips twitched. She quickly lifted a hand to her face and brushed her nose lightly to conceal the broad smile that threatened to reveal itself. She had to give Chester Symington credit for some intelligence.

The middle-aged, white-haired doyenne of Abilene's high society got up and went into the foyer. Mrs. Symington opened the door and stepped back to admit the visitor. "Why, Mr. Dixon!" she said. "How . . . how nice to see you." She was clearly baffled.

A burly, barrel-chested man stepped into the foyer, clutching his hat in his hands. Dressed in plain, clean, range clothes, he had a thick shock of gray hair, and his leathery face was tanned and lined. No one would guess that Hunter Dixon owned the largest ranch in this part of Kansas. He was wealthy enough to take it easy, but Aileen knew that he spent nearly every day working on the range right beside his cowhands.

"Howdy, Mrs. Symington," Dixon said with an awkward nod. He gazed into the parlor at the women plainly visible through the arched entrance. "Ladies."

Mrs. Symington had regained some of her composure. As she glanced down to make certain that Dixon had cleaned his boots, she said, "Won't you join us in the parlor, Mr. Dixon? It isn't often that a man participates in our meetings, but you're quite welcome, of course."

Dixon turned his hat over in his hands. Aileen could almost read his thoughts as he looked uncomfortably at the ladies gathered in the parlor. Clearly, he would rather face a gang of rustlers.

"I can't stay but a minute, ma'am," Dixon said to Mrs. Symington. "I knew you ladies would be planning the spring dance tonight, and I had something I wanted to say about it."

"Feel free, Mr. Dixon. We're all interested in anything you have to say, aren't we, ladies?"

Several women murmured their agreement.

Dixon nodded. "All right," he said abruptly. "I'll say it straight out. You ladies always invite the whole town and all the neighboring folks to that dance, don't you?"

"That's right, Mr. Dixon. It's a celebration for the entire community," Mrs. Symington pointed out.

"Well, me and the other ranchers think you ought to do it different this year. That bunch of squatters out on Doyle Needham's place shouldn't be welcome at the dance."

Dixon's words did not surprise Aileen. She had suspected that his objection to the settlers was the reason he had ventured into this female sanctum, especially after the trouble between Dixon's son and Tommy Parks a few days before. She decided to speak up. "Those settlers are part of the community, Mr. Dixon. They have a right to be part of any community function."

Dixon's cold eyes settled on her. "According to my son, Brice, they're troublemakers. We didn't ask them to come and take over good ranchland, Doctor."

Aileen felt the disapproving eyes of the other committee members boring into her as she glared at Dixon. She *was* a newcomer to the group, but she did not intend to back down.

"What actual harm are they doing to your ranch or any other, Mr. Dixon?" she asked bluntly.

"Needham's trying to fence off his range," Dixon snapped. "That land is next to mine. Our cattle have always used it when they needed to. Besides, if you let one bunch of farmers come in and take over open range, more will move in right behind them, looking to get rich off land that me and the other ranchers tamed!"

Aileen laughed and shook her head. "You obviously haven't been to visit any of those families, Mr. Dixon. If you had, you'd see that getting rich is the farthest thing from their minds. They're just trying to survive from one day to the next."

"Please, Dr. Bloom," Mrs. Symington said curtly. "We did not come here tonight to argue." She turned to the rancher. "I'm afraid you haven't given us a good reason to exclude any group from the dance, Mr. Dixon."

"Then how about this? Most of my ranch hands as well as riders from the other spreads will be at that dance. You let those farmers come, and there's bound to be trouble between them and the cowboys. You don't want a brawl, do you, Mrs. Symington?"

The woman pursed her lips sourly. "I thought we were trying to put all of that uncivilized behavior behind us, Mr. Dixon."

"I can't be responsible for what'll happen if they see those sodbusters there."

Mrs. Symington sighed. "I see."

So did Aileen. Dixon was delivering a warning. Keep the farmers away from the dance—or he would see to it that there was trouble.

"I believe you have a point after all, Mr. Dixon," Mrs. Symington said. She turned to the other women. "What do you think, ladies? We certainly don't want any disturbances to ruin the dance, do we?"

Aileen was not surprised that Mrs. Symington was giving in to Dixon's threat or that the other women agreed with her. Nevertheless, she refused to yield.

"It seems to me that the best way to avoid problems is to accept the newcomers as part of the community," she said quickly. Even as she spoke, she knew her words were futile.

Within moments, the committee had made a decision. The settlers from Georgia would not be invited to the annual spring dance. Hunter Dixon clapped his hat on his head and said, "Thank you, ladies," and quickly left.

Aileen put down her teacup and stood up. "I believe I had better be going, too," she said coolly.

"But we haven't finished our plans for the dance," Mrs. Symington protested.

Aileen smiled. "I'm afraid that doesn't seem to be my area of expertise," she said. "Thank you, anyway."

No one made any attempt to stop her as she said her good nights and left. Aileen knew it would be a long time before she was invited to another committee meeting.

But if what she had seen tonight was any indication of how Abilene's high society worked, that was all right with her.

The next day Luke Travis rode to the D Slash N and headed for the Parks farm. Over coffee early that morning, Aileen had told him about her previous evening's experience with the social committee and their decision about keeping the settlers from the dance. Travis had decided that the settlers needed to be informed. He was not sure that Isaac and the others would even care about being excluded, but they did need to know about the pressure Hunter Dixon was putting on other members of the community.

Travis also wanted to check on Tommy Parks. Since

the near-gunfight with Brice Dixon the week before, Tommy had not come into town, and Travis wanted to know if the young man was still packing a handgun. He hoped Tommy had finally put aside his anger and was behaving with some sense.

As the marshal approached the earthen cabin, he saw that Tommy and Isaac were both at work, repairing a broken plow handle. He was disappointed when he noticed the old Colt still strapped on Tommy's hip. Verna was washing clothes in a tub that sat under the canvas awning.

Travis dismounted and greeted the settlers. Isaac smiled and asked, "What brings you out here, Marshal?"

"Just wanted to see if you've had any more trouble," Travis replied lightly.

"Brice Dixon hasn't been around, if that's what you mean," Tommy said. "It's been pretty quiet."

"The cowboys seem to have gotten tired of bothering us again," Isaac added. "Maybe this time it'll last. Sooner or later they'll accept us, Luke. I'm convinced of that."

"Maybe." Travis looked uncomfortably at the man. "I'm not sure, though. Have you heard about the big dance they have every spring in Abilene?"

"Mr. Needham told us about it," Verna said. "It sounds like a lot of fun." A childlike smile of anticipation brightened her pretty face, making Travis realize sadly that this was one of the few times he had seen the young woman smile.

No point in postponing it, he decided. He broke the news to them, quickly explaining the decision of the social committee and the role Hunter Dixon had played in it. When he had finished, Travis glanced at the three hardworking settlers. Isaac looked disappointed, and Verna's eyes were flooded with tears. Anger darkened Tommy's face.

"That's not fair!" the young man cried. "They're inviting everybody in these parts 'cept us, aren't they?"

"I'm afraid so."

"Isn't there anything you can do, Marshal?" Verna pleaded.

Travis shrugged and shook his head. "No law's being broken," he explained as gently as he could. "The committee can invite anybody they want to. Since the dance is being held in a building owned by the town, you could attend. They can't keep you off public property."

"Then that's just what we'll do," Tommy declared.

Travis shook his head. "There'll be trouble if you do." He looked at the older man. "Isaac, I'm asking you to talk to the other settlers. I don't want another brawl in my town."

"Sounds to me like you're lettin' this Dixon fellow boss you around, Marshal," Tommy said harshly.

Travis stiffened. He looked pointedly at Tommy and said coldly, "I'm trying to keep law and order in Abilene. That's what I'm paid for. As long as nobody's breaking the law, I can't take sides, Tommy. You know that."

"We know, Luke," Isaac said at last. He had a thoughtful expression on his face. "And it's all right. I'll talk to the others. In fact, I've my own idea about how to handle this."

"Oh?" Travis said. "What's that?"

"What's to stop us from having our own dance?" he asked quietly. His blue eyes began to twinkle.

Slowly, a grin spread across Travis's face. "You just might have something there," the marshal said. "Yes, sir, you just might."

It was Saturday evening, two weeks after the run-in between Tommy Parks and Brice Dixon, and Cody Fisher was in the marshal's office getting ready for Abilene's spring dance. He stood before the small mirror that hung on the wall just outside of the cellblock and struggled with the top button of his white shirt. When he finally fastened it, he looped a string tie around his neck and shrugged into the jacket of his only suit. Running a finger around the tight shirt collar, he turned toward Luke Travis and grinned. "I tell you, Marshal, if it weren't for the ladies, I'd say that getting dressed up like this was a waste of time."

Travis was also wearing a suit and tie and, like Cody, had looped his gun belt around his waist. Neither lawman would be unarmed tonight, even though they were going to social functions.

"You'll survive, Cody," Travis said dryly. "Just keep your eyes open. I've sworn in a couple of extra deputies, but you'll be in charge."

Cody nodded. "I don't think things will get out of hand, but we'll be ready if they do. You just watch out while you're at Needham's place. I've got a bad feeling about that."

"So do I," Travis agreed. He moved to the pegs that hung on the wall next to the door and picked up his hat. "When Isaac first told me about it, I thought having a separate dance for the settlers was a good idea, but the more I've thought about it, the more worried I've gotten."

"I'm sure that Brice Dixon and his bunch of cowhands know about that party by now." Cody's face was grim as he looked at the marshal. "You sure you don't want me to ride out there with you?"

"I'm sure," Travis said. "I need you here in town. I can handle Brice and his friends if they show up and start trouble."

"Just be careful," Cody said quietly as he stared at Travis.

Travis laughed out loud. "I'm the one who's usually saying that to you. And you're the one who's going to be dancing with all the pretty young gals in town tonight."

Cody grinned. "That's right."

The lawmen walked out of the office together and mounted their horses. Cody swung his pinto down Texas Street to the east toward the courthouse, where Abilene's dance was being held.

With a wave to his deputy, Travis headed west. He was getting a later start than he had intended. The sun was already setting, sending purple and orange streaks across the deep blue Kansas sky. Travis hoped that nothing would happen before he reached Needham's ranch. Maybe nothing would happen at all tonight, and the settlers could simply enjoy their celebration. But every instinct Luke Travis had developed as a lawman told him that things would work out differently.

The settlers had been on Needham's ranch for nearly six weeks, and even though the cowboys were not harassing the farmers as regularly now, the hostility was still evident. Most of the townspeople also continued to be cool toward the newcomers. The efforts of Aileen, Judah, and Orion had done little to change the prevailing attitudes in Abilene.

Night had fallen by the time Travis reached Doyle Needham's ranch house. As he looked around the yard, he saw dozens of lanterns, some of them placed in the trees around the house, making the ranch a beacon in the darkness for miles around. The party was being held in the large open space between the house and barn. A buckboard was parked near the barn, and several men with fiddles and guitars stood in the wagon bed. They sawed and plucked at the instruments with vigor and enthusiasm, if not much talent. Quite a few couples were dancing to the music.

A great many wagons and saddle horses were tied up in front of the house. Travis put his mount among them and then spotted Doyle Needham and Isaac Parks standing at the end of the porch. From where they stood, they could watch the dancing while they smoked their pipes and talked.

Travis stepped onto the porch. Isaac and Needham nodded greetings to him, and Isaac said, "I'm glad you could make it, Marshal. How about some punch?"

Travis grinned. "What sort of ingredients does that concoction have, Isaac?"

"Well, it depends on which bowl you sample," he said with a chuckle.

Needham lifted a cup. "I recommend the one on the left, Travis."

Travis looked at the long table standing in the yard several feet away from the musicians' makeshift platform. Plates of food covered most of it, and two bowls of punch had been placed at the far end. Not surprisingly, the one on the left had the longest line of people in front of it.

"I'm glad you talked me into this fandango, Parks,"

Needham went on. "Figured it was nothing but foolishness at first, but danged if I'm not enjoyin' watchin' these folks have fun."

"Any trouble so far?" Travis asked.

"Not a bit," Isaac replied. "Nearly everyone is here tonight, and I think this is the best time we've had since we left Georgia. You're not expecting trouble, are you, Luke?"

How was he to explain the worry that gnawed at him? Travis wondered. There was no point in throwing cold water on the good time these people were having.

He chose to ignore Isaac's question and nodded toward the dancers. Tommy and Verna were swooping around. Like the musicians, they made up in enthusiasm what they lacked in practice. Travis said, "They make a fine-looking couple, don't they?"

"Indeed they do, Luke," Isaac murmured in agreement. "Indeed they do."

Needham drained his cup. "I could use a little more of that," he said. Travis and Isaac fell in beside him as he went down the porch steps and started toward the table.

It looked as if the dance was going to work out after all, Travis mused. Everyone seemed to be having a good time. The children were everywhere—running, laughing, and playing—and the adults beamed rare smiles as they danced. *If there are no other benefits from this party, Doyle Needham seems almost human tonight, and that's enough,* the marshal thought.

The sound of pounding hoofbeats stopped the three men before they could reach the punch bowls. Travis swung around and stared into the darkness beyond the pool of light cast by the lanterns. At the edge of the light, he saw the father of an arriving settler family suddenly swerve his buckboard to the side in an effort to get out of the way. The man's wife screamed in fright as a large group of riders thundered past the wagon into the ranch yard.

The newcomers brandished rifles and wore bandannas over their faces. One of the startled farmers jerked around and yelled, "Outlaws!" then leaped onto the porch to avoid being trampled.

Travis's hand flashed toward his gun. He palmed the Colt as the masked strangers yanked their mounts to a halt. As several men trained rifles on him, Travis froze, his gun not having cleared leather.

A large man who seemed to be leading the raiders shouted at the milling mob of frightened settlers. "Hold it! You sodbusters stand still, and nobody will get hurt!" He snapped his gaze on Travis and went on, "Drop that gun, mister, or we'll have to shoot you."

Slowly, Travis slid the Colt into its holster instead of dropping it as he had been ordered. He pushed back his coat to reveal the badge pinned to his vest. It gleamed in the lantern light.

"You'd better think twice about this," Travis advised coldly. A tense silence had fallen over the party, an abrupt contrast to the sounds of laughter and enjoyment that had filled the air only moments before. The musicians had lowered their instruments and fidgeted nervously.

The gang leader nudged his horse and walked the animal to where Travis stood motionless beside Isaac Parks and Doyle Needham. As the man approached, Travis could see dark eyes blazing under the brim of his black sombrero. Like the other riders, he wore a duster and gripped a Winchester menacingly in his hand. The bandanna was bright red and obscured the lower half of his face, but it was not large enough to conceal completely a bushy black beard.

Looking past the leader, Travis saw that the eighteen or nineteen men in the band were covering the entire crowd with their rifles. In a voice taut with tension, the marshal said, "What do you men want here?"

"Now that's an interesting question, Marshal," the spokesman for the raiders said. "I guess you could say we came to deliver a message."

"This is my place," Doyle Needham said harshly. "If you have a message for anyone, you might as well give it to me."

"Sure, mister." The bearded man dropped the barrel of his Winchester and blasted a slug into the ground between Needham's feet. Leaping backward, the stunned rancher lost his balance and would have fallen if Isaac had not grabbed his arm and steadied him.

Travis remained motionless, exerting every ounce of willpower not to reach for his gun. He knew he could take the leader of the masked men, but that would jeopardize every settler. At all costs, he had to maintain control.

The bearded man turned to the group of settlers. Lifting his voice, he boomed, "We heard about you squatters and came to see what we could do to put matters right! You people have no place on cattle range!"

"These folks aren't squatters," Travis said coldly. "They have a legal right to be on this land and to use it for farming or anything they choose."

The man glanced at Travis, his glittering eyes unreadable, then went on, "You sodbusters have been killing cattle that don't belong to you and denying the ranchers their legal right to have access to water and graze for their stock. We've come to put a stop to that and to see that the rights of the ranchers are enforced!"

Travis had not expected a disturbance like this. Some rowdy cowboys . . . perhaps, but examining this crew of hardcases, he knew they were not from the Abilene area. What were hired guns doing here?

"That's a lie!" Isaac called out. "We've killed no cattle. And the only fences that have been put up are on Mr. Needham's land. There's nothing illegal about it."

"Maybe that's what you think, old man. But that's not the way the ranchers see it. They've got rights, too."

"Enforcing the law and making sure that everyone is treated fairly is my job," Travis said.

The man grunted, lifted the bottom of his bandanna, and spat contemptuously. "Doesn't look like you're doing a very good job of it, Marshal. Otherwise you wouldn't be out here taking part in this little shindig."

Before Travis could reply, Isaac walked toward the man's horse and said, "The marshal is here because he was invited, mister. And now you are, too."

Stunned, both Travis and Needham looked at him as if he had lost his mind. The leader of the riders uttered an incredulous, "What?"

"You're invited to join us, you and your friends. There's good music and dancing and some fine punch. So why don't you join the festivities?"

Tommy Parks cried, "Pa! What—"

Isaac waved his son into silence. "How about it?" he said, looking up at the bearded man.

Finally, the man shook his head. "You are one crazy old coot," he muttered. Looking back at Travis, he went on, "I reckon these people know what we want. They're to get out of these parts as soon as possible, or suffer the consequences. In the meantime, my men and I will be patrolling the area, and we won't stand for any trouble from sodbusters." He urged his horse forward. "And just so you don't forget—"

The animal pushed against the table piled high with food and punch bowls as the man reached down and grabbed its edge. In a single movement, the table overturned with a gigantic crash, scattering food and breaking plates and bowls. The children wailed in protest, and their mothers sobbed.

The rest of the raiders suddenly tilted their rifles and started firing into the night sky. As they boomed their weapons into the blackness, they spurred their horses and galloped out of the circle of light, vanishing into the darkened Kansas prairie.

Doyle Needham raged a torrent of profanity at the cloud of dust the raiders left in their wake. The settler men rushed to Needham, Travis, and Isaac, clamoring to know what they planned to do about this new threat. Any thought of continuing the party was abandoned. The women had begun to collect their children and herd them into the wagons.

"Quiet!" Travis roared. "Quiet, please." When the clamor around him subsided, he said, "You men go on home. I don't think anything else will happen tonight, but keep your eyes open anyway."

Grumbling and disappointed, the settlers boarded their wagons and rolled away from Needham's ranch house, scattering to the soddies they had built. Travis and Isaac watched them go. Saying he needed a real drink, Needham stalked into the house.

"What do you think, Marshal?" Isaac asked.

Travis considered his answer for a moment. He was well aware that Tommy was standing nearby. The young man was furious at what had happened tonight.

That was understandable, Travis thought. He had a burr under the saddle himself. "Those weren't just cowhands out to have a good time," he said. "I'm not sure who they were or what they really want, but I intend to find out."

"They looked like they meant business," Isaac said dryly.

Tommy said, "I don't think any of us should go anywhere from now on without havin' a gun with us."

That suggestion came as no surprise to Travis, and he could not dispute Tommy's logic. The situation was now more dangerous than ever.

"Stay close to home, and be alert," Travis said. "I'll be looking into this."

"Look hard, Marshal," Tommy said coldly, "before too many folks get killed."

Chapter Ten

————◆————

DURING THE LONG RIDE BACK TO ABILENE, LUKE TRAVIS thought about what had happened and tried to come up with a plan to keep the trouble from getting worse. With the arrival of these new raiders, the situation had become intolerable.

As had been pointed out to him, Needham's ranch was outside his jurisdiction. Friendship for Isaac Parks and a desire to maintain peace in Abilene had motivated his actions. But he could legally wash his hands of the whole affair and simply throw anyone who made trouble in town, cowhand and sodbuster alike, into jail.

Even as the thought crossed his mind, Travis knew he could not operate that way. He had always worked on the side of justice, and he could not close his eyes now.

As he crossed the bridge over Mud Creek and

walked his horse into town, he could hear the merry strains of music coming from the courthouse at the other end of Texas Street. Normally bustling with relaxing cowboys on a Saturday night, the street was deserted, a sure sign to Travis that the dance was still in full swing. Seeing that no one was waiting for him at the marshal's office, Travis continued on to the courthouse and tied up his horse.

Several groups of men stood on the lawn around the stately building, talking and passing flasks back and forth. Some of them nodded and said hello as the marshal walked toward the front door. He returned the greetings and stepped through the doorway into the brightly lit hall, taking off his hat as he did so.

Quite a few couples filled the floor, which had been cleared of chairs for the occasion. The small platform where the town council usually sat was now a bandstand. The musicians who stood there and played were more skilled than their counterparts at the settlers' dance and matched them in enthusiasm. Everyone appeared to be having a fine time.

Scanning the crowd, Travis noticed Cody standing near the table where the punch bowls sat. He had a cup in his hand and was smiling as he sipped it and watched the dancers.

Travis saw Aileen Bloom dancing with a tall, burly, bearded man. Recognizing the man as Leslie Gibson, the town's new schoolteacher, the marshal grimaced. He had heard about Gibson and his prizefighting past from Cody and Orion, and the newcomer's athletic ability was apparent from the graceful way he moved as he danced.

Stifling an unfamiliar twinge of jealousy, Travis

decided that Aileen could dance with whomever she pleased. He liked and admired the doctor, but the two of them were only friends. Nevertheless, at that moment he wished she was in *his* arms, moving like a dream to the spirited music.

Shaking his head, he started around the edge of the room, heading toward Cody. He had more important things to think about than who was dancing with whom.

Cody saw him coming and grinned. "No trouble, Marshal," he announced as Travis walked up to him. "Everything's been quiet."

"That's good," Travis replied. "I'm surprised you're not dancing. I figured Agnes Hirsch would have worn your boots down to bare feet by now."

Cody laughed. "She's been trying, and so have some of the other ladies. I'm just resting before I go back out there."

Travis gestured at the punch cup in the deputy's hand. "Anybody try to spike that?"

"No. That's going on outside."

Travis remembered the men standing outside the building and nodded. "As long as they don't start any trouble, I don't mind." One of the dancers caught his eye. "I see Hunter Dixon is here."

Cody glanced at the barrel-chested rancher, who was whirling a local widow around the dance floor. Dixon's wife had passed away several years earlier, and he was regarded as a prime catch by the unattached, middle-aged women of the town. "He's been here all evening," Cody said. "Most of the other ranchers are around, too."

"I've been wondering about that," Travis said thoughtfully.

Cody looked sharply at him. "Something happen out at Needham's?"

"Let's go outside, and I'll tell you about it."

Cody put his cup on the table and followed Travis through the back door of the building. Once outside, the marshal quickly told Cody about the masked riders disrupting the farmers' dance.

"Dixon's men have been here the whole time," Cody said when Travis was finished. "Brice, too. So it couldn't have been them. Do you think they were some cowhands from one of the other spreads?"

Travis shook his head. "I don't think so. They didn't act like cowhands on a tear. They were out to do more than throw a scare into those settlers. Given the least excuse, they would have shot up the place."

"And if a lawman hadn't been there," Cody speculated.

"I imagine you're right. We were lucky tonight, Cody. I've got a feeling that as long as those men are in the area, things are just going to get worse."

"Sounds to me like they're hired guns brought in by the ranchers."

"That's the impression I got, too," Travis agreed. "I think I'll ride out to the Rafter D next week and have a word with Hunter Dixon."

"He's inside. Why not tonight?"

Travis shook his head. "I don't want to spoil the dance. And Dixon's just the type to get his back up and make a scene. I'd rather talk to him at his ranch." Travis ran a tired hand over his face. "Why don't you go on back inside and enjoy what's left of the dance?"

"What are you going to do?"

"Go to the office. I've got some thinking to do."

Cody nodded. "All right." He forced a grin. "We'll get it all sorted out sooner or later."

Travis wished he could be that optimistic.

As the deputy returned to the party through the rear door, Travis walked across the broad lawn surrounding the courthouse toward the street. As he reached the boardwalk, a laughing couple strolled arm in arm out of the front door of the courthouse.

Travis heard his name and turned to see Aileen Bloom and Leslie Gibson. In the light spilling out from inside, Travis could see that Aileen's smiling face was flushed from the dancing. She had never looked prettier, he thought.

"Hello, Luke," Aileen said merrily. "Have you met Leslie Gibson, the new schoolteacher?"

"Not formally." Travis extended his hand to the big man. "I've seen you around, Mr. Gibson. You're hard to miss."

Leslie returned the firm grip. "So are you, Marshal. I'm glad to meet you. Dr. Bloom has been singing your praises all evening long."

Travis glanced coolly at Aileen, whose blush deepened. "I just told Leslie about some of the things that have happened since you came to Abilene, Luke."

"It has been eventful," Travis admitted dryly.

"We came outside for a breath of fresh air," the teacher said. "Aren't you coming into the dance, Marshal?"

"I've been inside to speak with Cody. I've got to go to the office now." Travis lightly slapped his thigh. "I picked up some buckshot in this leg not long ago. Don't know if it'd be a good idea to do any dancing just yet."

"Well, Luke, as your doctor, I can assure you that a dance or two isn't going to affect your injury," Aileen said.

Travis smiled. "Maybe not, but I really do have some work to do." He turned to Leslie. "I am curious, though, about how you're getting along with Thurman Simpson, Mr. Gibson."

Leslie laughed, a deep, booming sound. "We haven't killed each other yet, Marshal. I guess that's something. Let's just say that we have different philosophies when it comes to educating children."

The man certainly did not sound like a former bare-knuckle brawler, Travis thought. Slugger Gibson, that was what Orion had called him.

"I wish you luck, Mr. Gibson," Travis said. He put on his hat and extended his hand to Leslie again.

"Good night, Luke," Aileen said as he strolled to the hitchrack.

"Good night," he called back.

As he rode to the office, he put thoughts of Aileen and Leslie Gibson out of his mind and concentrated on the settlers' problems. Dismounting, he ambled into the office and lit the fire under the coffee. He was certain it would be a long night.

Travis tossed his hat on a peg and shrugged out of his coat. When the coffee was ready, he poured a steaming cupful, sat down at his desk, and pulled a thick sheaf of papers from the top drawer. The documents were wanted posters and law enforcement circulars he had received during the last several months.

In less than an hour, Travis found what he wanted. He spread the circular in front of him and examined it once more. The description matched, even though there was no picture to verify it.

According to the document, the man called B. W. Royal was known to be operating as a hired enforcer for ranchers throughout the West. Over the last few years, he had ranged from Texas to Montana Territory. Royal had had numerous brushes with the law and was implicated in a suspicious fire that had wiped out a sodbuster family in Nebraska, but no warrants had been issued for his arrest. The circular merely alerted lawmen to be on the lookout for Royal in their vicinity.

Travis, his expression bleak, pushed the paper away and sat back in his chair. He was fairly sure the man who had led the raid on Needham's ranch had been B. W. Royal. Royal would not be here in Kansas unless someone had hired him and his crew of hardcases. The stakes had gone up tonight. Now somebody was playing for blood.

Over the next few days, the marshal's worries about B. W. Royal and his hired men became a reality. Reports reached him of new raids on the tenant farms at Needham's D Slash N. At first the settlers were merely harassed, much as they had been when they first arrived. Then the attacks became steadily more serious. More crops were destroyed, more animals were killed, and at least one soddy was razed after its interior was gutted by a fire started on the thatched roof. The men who brought this destruction were always masked and struck at night.

Royal was staying busy, Travis thought as he seethed in frustration.

He knew the bearded man and his companions were camped somewhere nearby, but several forays into the countryside had not unearthed the gang. The time had come, Travis decided, to visit Hunter Dixon and demand some answers.

On the morning the marshal reached the decision, he was sitting at his desk, finishing a cup of coffee, when Cody burst through the door.

"Isaac Parks is coming down Texas Street in his wagon, Marshal," Cody said in a rush. "Tommy's with him, and they both look like something terrible has happened."

Travis stood up and followed Cody onto the boardwalk. He looked west and spotted the wagon driven by Isaac and beside it Tommy, on horseback. Even at this distance, Travis clearly saw their grim expressions.

He stepped into the street and walked quickly to meet them. Isaac hauled on the lines, bringing the wagon to a stop, as Travis approached. Not bothering with formalities, the lawman simply asked, "What's wrong, Isaac?"

"We've got Ed Morton in the back, Marshal," Isaac said heavily. "He's dead."

Travis stared at the sheet-covered form in the wagon bed. He was vaguely aware that Cody now stood beside him, tense and ready for trouble. In a voice he barely knew as his own, Travis said, "What happened?"

"Those damn night riders killed him, that's what happened," Tommy Parks said hotly. The young man's eyes blazed with anger. "They came up to his place last night, yellin' and shootin' and scarin' his wife and kids to death. Ed never was one to take that.

He ran outside when they started throwin' torches on the roof of his soddy. He had a shotgun in his hands, so they just cut him down, Travis. The man never had a chance!"

"The boy's right, Luke," Isaac said. "We got the story from Bessie Morton. Verna's with her and the children at what's left of their place." He looked more haggard than ever as he shook his head and went on, "I don't know what they'll do now that Ed's gone. It's going to be bad for them."

Travis took a deep breath, outrage at this senseless killing surging through him. He had been afraid that something like this would happen. That no one had been killed before this was only pure luck.

"I'm going to put a stop to this, Isaac," Travis said icily. "I don't know how, but I'll find a way."

"That's mighty fine," Tommy snapped, "but it's a little late for Ed, isn't it?"

Trying to ignore the angry words, Travis turned to Cody. "Take them to the undertaker. Tell him that the town's paying for the funeral. If the council doesn't like it, I'll pay for it myself."

"You won't do it alone," Cody said. He nodded toward the boardwalk.

Several men and women stood on the boardwalk silently staring at the lawmen and the wagon. From the shocked expressions on their faces, they had obviously heard the news about Ed Morton's murder. No one jeered or hurled insults now. Violent death, the tragedy of a family left on its own, had opened a few eyes, Travis thought.

The word would spread through town. By noon, everyone would know that the mysterious night riders had killed a man. Some would say that Ed Morton was only a sodbuster and, as such, did not matter, but others would understand. Understand—and maybe change a little.

The marshal turned and started toward his horse. "I'm going to Dixon's place," he said over his shoulder to Cody.

He stopped at the office to pick up his hat, then swung onto his horse and rode northwest out of Abilene. The ride to Dixon's Rafter D would take about an hour; by the time he reached the ranch, he might have calmed down a little. Somehow, though, Travis doubted it.

The marshal had been on Dixon's range for fifteen minutes before the ranch headquarters—a large two-story frame house with a soddy nestled on the rise behind it—came into view. That soddy had been Hunter Dixon's home when he first started the Rafter D. As he and the ranch prospered, he had built the house for his wife and only son.

When several cowhands working the range on either side of the trail spotted the marshal, they turned from their chores and rode toward him. The grim-faced men kept about fifty yards away but paralleled his progress toward the ranch house. Travis turned in his saddle and noticed that two men had fallen in behind him. He was ringed by a hostile escort, and the anger he had nurtured during his journey was now coupled with a malignant tension.

Travis rode up to the house. As the cowhands sat on their mounts in the ranch yard and watched in silence, he swung down from his horse, stepped onto the porch, and knocked on the door. A moment later, the door was opened by Hunter Dixon himself. He frowned when he saw Abilene's marshal standing there with a grim look on his lean face.

One of the cowboys called, "This man's trespassin', boss. You want us to run him off?"

Dixon shook his head and waved the punchers away. "You boys get back to work," he growled. "I'll handle this." As the hands returned to their chores, Dixon regarded Travis speculatively. "What can I do for you, Marshal?"

"I suppose you've heard about the new trouble those farmers on Needham's ranch are having," Travis said.

"I've heard a little," Dixon said with a shrug. "It's none of my business, though. I've got worries of my own just running this spread."

Travis watched the rancher intently, looking for any signs of lying or guilt. "What do you know about a man called B. W. Royal?"

Dixon's eyes narrowed. "I've heard of him. Some sort of hired gun, ain't he?"

"That's exactly what he is. And he's been known to work for ranchers who want some sodbusters out of the way."

Dixon's jaw tightened and a red flush crept over his face. "You accusin' me of hirin' this man Royal, Marshal? I didn't even know he was around here."

Despite what appeared to be genuine anger, the words did not ring true to Travis. He said, "Royal's around, all right. I saw him myself at Needham's, the night of the dance. And I've had several reports of a man fitting his description leading raids on the farms the last few nights."

"But you don't know for sure it's Royal, do you?" Dixon asked shrewdly.

"I don't have proof," Travis admitted.

"And even if it is, you sure don't know who hired him, right?" A smug smile played around the rancher's wide mouth.

Travis suppressed the impulse to smash a fist into that expression. "Like I said, I don't have any proof."

"Well, it wasn't me, Marshal. I can't speak for anybody else."

"You'd better be damned sure of that, Dixon. Because a man was killed last night, and B. W. Royal and his men were the ones who did it."

Breath hissed between Dixon's gritted teeth. "I was goin' to invite you in for a cup of coffee, Travis, but I don't think I will now. I fight my own battles, mister. I never in my life paid anybody to gun down somebody else."

The two men glared angrily at each other on the porch, and they both jerked around when the screen door of the house banged open.

Brice Dixon strode out. His face was red with fury, and his hand hung close to the butt of his gun. "I heard that, you son of a bitch!" he raged at Travis. "You can't accuse my pa of something like that and get away with it."

"Brice!" Dixon lashed out angrily. Moving quickly, he stepped between his son and Travis. "Stop it, you fool! Travis is a lawman."

"I don't care! He can't talk to you like that!"

Dixon gripped Brice's shoulders and bodily steered

him to the door. "Get back in that house! I'll handle this." He yanked the door open, shoved Brice inside, and closed it after him.

A fine sheen of sweat glistened on Dixon's forehead when he turned back to Travis. "Boy flies off the handle too easy," he said.

"Thanks for stepping in. I didn't want him drawing on me."

Dixon looked meaningfully at Travis. "I didn't want *you* drawing on *him.*" He squared his shoulders. "Look, Travis, unless you've got something else to say, I think you'd better get off my land. I've told you I don't have anything to do with B. W. Royal or one of those sodbusters getting killed. There's nothing more to say."

"Okay," Travis said. With a curt nod, he went to his horse, mounted up, and rode away from the ranch house.

Travis was still not convinced that Hunter Dixon knew nothing about the hired guns coming to Abilene. This visit to Rafter D might still have some results, the marshal hoped as he swung away from the main trail and rode into the trees and brush of a hedgerow.

The clump of brush was on a slight rise, and in its protective cover, he could sit unobserved and see the ranch house. As far as he could tell, no one was paying any attention to him; Dixon's cowhands had moved to work elsewhere on the huge spread. Travis waited for a half hour, watching to see if either Dixon left the house.

If the Dixons did have some connection with B. W. Royal, they would want to warn the man that Travis knew who he was. Sometimes the only way to get the results you wanted was to stir up a hornet's nest, the lawman mused.

He was about to give up when Brice Dixon rushed from the house and hurried to the corral. The young man quickly saddled a horse, swung onto the animal, and galloped away from the ranch house, heading south.

Behind him, at a good distance, rode Luke Travis.

Chapter Eleven

ABOUT TWO MILES SOUTH OF THE RANCH HOUSE, BRICE Dixon suddenly turned onto a small track that ran southeast of the main trail. The countryside was brushy and rugged, and Travis realized that they were moving into an area where several small creeks flowed into the Solomon River.

As he trailed Brice, Travis passed a few small herds of grazing cattle, and he supposed they were still on the Rafter D range. He had given Brice a good quarter-mile head start, and the young man was in a big hurry, so the marshal knew he would not be spotted. Brice forded one stream, but at the next he turned and followed the creek to the east. Travis closed the gap between himself and the young man, wanting to hear Brice's conversation with Royal when he finally reached his destination.

A few moments later Brice rode into a stand of trees and thick brush. Travis could smell the rich aroma of coffee heating over a campfire and reined in before he reached the thicket. He dismounted quickly, walking his horse away from the trail and into the scrubby hedgerow.

After tying his horse to a small bush, Travis silently picked his way among the trees and thick brush. A man like Royal would post sentries, and Travis wanted to avoid them at all costs. Slithering behind every bit of available cover, he approached close enough to part the brush a little and peer into the encampment.

Travis studied the large camp, which had been set up in a wide clearing. A few tents were pitched close to the creek, and several bedrolls were spread around a crackling fire. Grazing in a makeshift corral, formed by ropes strung between trees, were two dozen horses. Ten men dozed in the cool shade of the trees, while another six or seven were busy cleaning weapons and repairing saddles. One man held the reins of Brice Dixon's horse. Brice had dismounted and now stood in front of the largest tent, talking animatedly with a heavyset man who sported a bushy black beard.

As he listened to Brice, the man paced impatiently and turned to face Travis's hiding place. The same glittering blue eyes Travis had seen a few nights earlier at the settlers' dance flashed across the clearing.

B. W. Royal, Travis thought. *It has to be.*

Travis was not close enough to hear most of what Brice was saying, but he did catch an occasional word or phrase—"lawman," "knows who . . . are," and "goddamn Travis!" He grinned humorlessly. *I was right,* he thought. *Hunter Dixon sent his son to warn Royal that I know who he is.*

Royal's booming laughter reached Travis, and then

the bearded outlaw shook his head and clapped the worried-looking younger man on the shoulder.

Brice twisted from Royal's grasp, said something angrily, then turned and stalked to his horse. He yanked the reins away from the man holding them, mounted, and galloped out of the camp.

As he fled, the enraged young man passed less than thirty yards from the marshal's hiding place. Well concealed, Travis nevertheless crouched deeper in the brush, although Brice was far too angry to notice anything.

Travis took a deep breath. Royal had laughed off Brice's warning and was obviously not afraid of some local lawman. Travis knew from the circular he had read that the burly, bearded man was used to riding where he wanted and doing as he pleased.

When the hoofbeats of Brice's horse had faded away, Travis slipped out of his hiding place and went to his horse. He swung into the saddle.

Now that he knew where Royal and his men were camped, he could go back to Abilene for help before he paid a formal visit to the bearded man. But what would that accomplish? Travis asked himself. Despite his certainty that the man was responsible for the atrocities of the last few days, he had no proof. Nor was Royal wanted anywhere else. Travis had no grounds on which to arrest him.

The marshal turned his horse toward the camp. Maybe some straight talk would do some good.

As he rode through the trees, he heard a low whistle, undoubtedly a guard's signal, and grimaced knowingly. He had been lucky that they had not spotted him before.

Slowly walking his horse into the camp, Travis

scanned the group of rough-looking men. All of them stood grimly tensed with their weapons held ready. They did not drop their guard when they saw that he was alone.

B. W. Royal, still standing in front of his tent, arrogantly assessed him with icy, piercing eyes. His hand rested on the butt of the Remington revolver holstered at his waist. Travis rode directly up to him, reined in, and looked down at him. "B. W. Royal?" he asked.

"What if I am?" the bearded man responded.

Travis felt the hostile eyes of the men boring into him. The badge pinned on his vest was like a red flag to hardcases like these.

"I'm Luke Travis, the marshal of Abilene. I thought it might be a good idea if we had a talk."

Royal looked shrewdly at him. "I'm not wanted for anything, and neither are any of my men."

Travis doubted the last part of that statement, but he was not going to press the point. "I'm here to talk, not to arrest anybody," he responded.

A flicker of a smile played at Royal's lips. "Light and set, then, Marshal. You already know I'm B. W. Royal."

The marshal dismounted slowly, not wanting to spook any of the gunmen. A chill ran through Travis, and he realized he had been a fool to ride in here alone. But turning to face Royal, he concealed his apprehension and said evenly, "I want law and order in my town, mister. I won't stand for anybody making trouble."

"Now, have we done anything in Abilene, Marshal? My boys and I haven't even been into town."

"I know that," Travis said with a nod. "But you're

raising a ruckus in the area, and that's going to affect Abilene. We've had enough trouble between the farmers and the ranch hands in town. I want this situation to cool down, not get hotter. I want it to stop."

Royal shook his head. "You're talking to the wrong man, Marshal. I don't even know what you're talking about. My friends and I are just resting our horses for a few days."

"On Hunter Dixon's range? Does he know about that, Royal?"

"Are we on the Rafter D?" Royal asked casually. "I heard of Dixon but didn't know this was his land."

"His son was just here," Travis said coldly.

For an instant, anger flickered in Royal's blue eyes, anger at Brice Dixon for allowing himself to be followed, Travis reasoned. The bearded man said, "You talking about that pup who rode in a few minutes ago? I don't know anything about him, Marshal. Never saw him before today."

"And I suppose you didn't have anything to do with a farmer being killed last night," Travis snapped. He heard several guns being cocked, an unmistakable sound that would make any man's spine go cold, no matter how brave—or crazy—he was.

Royal grinned. "We're peace-loving men, Marshal. You'd have to have mighty strong proof to show that we've bothered anybody since we've been here."

"You disrupted that dance at Needham's place," Travis pointed out. "I was there. I saw you."

"Did you see the face of any man here?" Royal shot back.

"You know I didn't. All of you wore masks, just like you did when you killed Ed Morton." Travis laughed contemptuously. "Wearing masks because you were afraid to show your faces."

Madness glittered in Royal's eyes, and the marshal tensed. *If Royal goes for his gun, I'll kill him,* he thought. *I'll never leave alive, but then neither will Royal.*

The fire in the gang leader's eyes suddenly died. He threw back his head and laughed, in the same way he had laughed at Brice Dixon. "You don't know a damned thing, Marshal," he declared. "You're just spouting words to see where they land. Now why don't you ride back to Abilene and stop harassing law-abiding citizens?"

Travis looked at him for a long moment. "When I get the evidence I need, I'll be back to see you, Royal."

The bearded man laughed again. "Always glad to see a representative of law and order, Marshal."

As he mounted up, Travis saw that the other men had formed a tight ring around him. He turned his horse and rode toward them, his face stony. With a slight nod from Royal, the grim-faced hardcases stepped back and allowed Travis through. He kept the horse at a steady walk until he was on the open trail, then heeled it into a trot.

When he was half a mile away from the camp, he raised a shaking hand to wipe the cold sweat off his forehead. He had come close to dying back there, and he knew it.

He doubted he had done any good by his visit; at best he had put Royal and his men on notice. They knew that he was aware of their identities and would look for proof of their crimes, but he did not believe that they would pack up and leave.

As he rode toward Abilene, pondering his next move, some instinct alerted him. With a frown, he reined in, his keen eyes scanning the rolling, brushy countryside around him.

The glint of sunlight on metal flashed in a clump of trees fifty yards ahead to his left. Acting reflexively, he kicked his feet free of the stirrups and dove from the saddle. A bullet whistled over his head, followed a second later by the flat crack of a rifle.

Landing hard on the ground, the marshal rolled and came up with his hand darting to his holstered Colt. His horse, spooked by the shot, danced around nervously between him and the thicket where he had spotted the reflection.

Another weapon blasted, this time from the other side of the trail. Travis was completely exposed to that assailant, and as a slug kicked up dust a few feet away from him, he burst into a run. To his left were a few trees, and though they would provide scant protection, Travis took two steps toward them. Then suddenly he stopped and whirled around.

The guns of both ambushers roared, the bullets whining through the sparse thicket where the men thought Travis would take cover. His feint had worked. Taking advantage of the few seconds the trick had bought him, he raced toward his horse.

The image of Pony Express riders vaulting onto their mounts flashed in his mind, and he decided to try that maneuver. Instead of a few moments being shaved off an express run, however, his life hung in the balance.

The horse had started to trot anxiously down the trail toward home, and Travis had to sprint, gun in hand, to catch up to the animal. He jammed the Colt into its holster. Timing his leap and setting his hands on the horse's rump, he launched himself forward into the saddle.

Immediately, he hunched against the horse's neck and dug his spurs into its side. Travis did not believe in treating his animals roughly, but he needed all the speed the horse could give. The animal lunged, racing between the two ambushers.

Glimpsing one man trying to aim his rifle, Travis palmed out the Colt and fired before the man had time to get off a shot. The slug slammed into the man's middle, knocking him backward and doubling him over, the rifle spinning from his hands as he collapsed.

Despite the lucky shot, Travis was still in danger. Even as he twisted in the saddle to locate the second man, a Winchester cracked. An unseen hand plucked the hat from Travis's head.

He triggered off two quick shots as he passed the stand of brush where the man was hidden. Then he hauled on the reins and wheeled his horse around. In the sudden silence that fell, he heard a shouted curse, followed by the sound of hoofbeats.

Flickering movement caught his eye. A third man? Or the second one fleeing?

Travis held his fire, edged cautiously toward the thick brush, and searched the hedgerow through narrowed eyes. The second ambusher was gone. On the ground, he noticed a splash of red.

One of his shots had found its target, Travis thought grimly as he looked down at the fresh blood. He had wounded the man and scared him off.

Travis rode back to the trail and retrieved his hat,

grimacing at the ragged bullet hole in its crown. He walked to the first man, who lay motionless on the dusty ground. The gunman was on his side, eyes open and staring sightlessly. The widening pool of blood beneath him seeped from the wound high in his belly.

The marshal looked thoughtfully toward B. W. Royal's camp. By riding hard and circling around, his attacker's could have left there and gotten in front of him. Travis did not recognize the man he had killed, but that did not mean anything. With his wolfish, beard-stubbled face and dusty range clothes, the dead man could easily have been one of the many hardcases at the camp.

If Royal had sent this man after him, Travis abruptly decided, then Royal should get him back.

A few minutes spent scouting through the brush turned up the slain ambusher's horse, which Travis brought back to the body and tied to a bush. The horse snorted and tried to dance away when it smelled the corpse, and its eyes were wide and fearful when the marshal draped the body over the saddle.

Leading the horse bearing the dead man, Travis rode toward Royal's camp. Unless the second ambusher, the one who had escaped, had already returned, Royal was in for a surprise. The marshal, his anger overriding any sense of caution, rode boldly up to the stand of trees that encircled the camp and started through them.

"Hold it, mister!" demanded a strident voice. Travis reined in as a sentry, menacingly pointing a rifle, stepped from behind a tree.

"I brought something back for Royal," Travis said

coldly. He nodded toward the grisly burden on the second horse.

The guard motioned with his rifle. "Go ahead," he said. "But I'll be right behind you, so don't try anything."

Spurring his horse to a walk, Travis laughed harshly. He was not likely to do anything foolish in Royal's stronghold. On the other hand, coming back here with a dead man was not the smartest thing he had ever done. But he could not allow Royal to get away with such tactics, and he wanted the gang leader to know it.

As he rode in, an excited hubbub ran through the camp. Royal's men came out of their tents and sprang from their sleeping bags. All of them pointed weapons at him. No one betrayed any knowledge of the dead man, but that came as no surprise. Royal would have trained them not to reveal any secrets.

Travis headed straight for the large tent. Royal knew that something was happening, because he thrust aside the tent flap and strode into the sunlight. His hands rested lightly on his hips, only inches from the gun and knife he wore, and an arrogant grin beamed on his bearded face. For a fleeting moment, however, Travis sensed shock flash in the big man's eyes. Royal had probably thought that sending two men after the marshal would do the job.

Travis stopped a few feet in front of Royal and pulled the other horse up. Grasping the dead man's collar, he yanked the body from the saddle and let it slide heavily to the ground.

"I figured you must have lost this, Royal," Travis said icily.

The bearded man seemed to quiver with rage,

telling Travis that the dead man was indeed one of Royal's crew. But after a moment Royal took a deep breath and said, "I never saw this man before in my life, Marshal."

"You're willing to swear to that?"

"Of course I am. He's a total stranger."

"And your men have never seen him, either." Travis's words were a statement, not a question.

"Reckon not. Did any of them speak up when you brought him in?"

Travis shook his head.

"Well, there you are, then. My men believe in speaking their minds. They'd have let you know if they knew this man."

Travis did not believe that. Royal was clearly in charge, and his men would follow his lead. That was one of the things keeping Travis alive right now. Royal had yet to make a move against him, so his men were biding their time.

"I don't like ambushes, Royal," Travis said. "You'd better bury this man. You'll have another one coming in soon who'll be carrying some lead. You might want to tend to him, too."

"We'll be glad to bury this stranger, Marshal. It's our Christian duty, after all. And we always help anybody who shows up at our campfire in trouble."

Travis wanted to shove the arrogant words down Royal's throat. He was sick and tired of this game. Not saying anything more, he turned and rode out of the camp.

He had a feeling that this time he would reach Abilene without any trouble. Royal had tried to get rid of him once today and failed. The man struck Travis as the type who would wait and carefully plan his next move. One thing was sure—Royal would not let what Travis had done go unavenged.

The marshal knew the showdown with B. W. Royal was inevitable. Given everything that had happened since Royal and his men had arrived, that showdown could not come soon enough for Luke Travis.

Chapter Twelve

JUDAH FISHER WEARILY SHRUGGED OUT OF HIS COAT AND tossed it over the back of a pew. The Wednesday-evening service had ended an hour earlier, and he was alone in the darkened church. He had extinguished all but one lamp, which burned near the pulpit.

He had delivered a short, hopeful sermon that evening, preaching the importance of understanding and compassion for one's fellowman despite his differences. The parishioners had complimented Judah on the sermon, but he feared that no matter how many times he preached those ideas, the town would never fully accept the Georgia settlers. No longer newcomers, the farmers were still greeted coolly whenever they came to Abilene. Now a new group of night riders was inflaming the hostility.

Cody had told him about Marshal Travis's visit to B. W. Royal's camp the day before. Judah was not surprised that the gang leader had arrogantly denied his crimes; too many men refused responsibility for their actions.

The situation preyed on Judah's mind as he swept out the sanctuary following the service. Boys from the orphanage often helped with such chores, but tonight Judah wanted to be alone to think.

He sank heavily into a pew and sighed. A rational man, he prided himself on being able to find a solution to almost any problem, but wrestling with this for weeks had produced nothing but frustration.

The creaking of the church door startled Judah. He turned to peer into the shadows at the back of the sanctuary and called, "Who's there?"

"Preacher?" said an unfamiliar man's voice. "That you?"

"I'm Judah Fisher, the pastor of this church. Can I help you?" As the stranger edged tentatively into the church, Judah could see that he wore overalls and clutched a battered hat.

"Name's Zeke Fimple, Preacher. I come in from Needham's place."

Judah stood up. "Of course, I remember you now," he said, although the man looked only vaguely familiar. "How are you, Zeke?"

"Reckon I'm all right," Fimple replied. "Didn't come about myself, though. I . . . I come to find some help for my brother, Matt."

"What's wrong with him?"

"Them fellers in the masks, they come to our place tonight." Fimple's voice began to break. "They hauled Matt out of the soddy and beat the hell outta him, Preacher! P-pardon my talk, but I got to have some help for him."

"That's all right," Judah said soothingly. He moved

quickly to the man's side and grasped his arm. "Your brother was badly hurt, you said?"

Fimple nodded. "Yeah. They all hit him and kicked him. . . . I was afraid to fight back. Lord, I'm so ashamed—"

"Was anyone else hurt?" Judah asked.

The man shook his head. "Just Matt. I knew he needed help, and I recollected Isaac Parks sayin' that you were his friend. I thought maybe you could . . ."

Judah nodded. "Of course. We'll go find the doctor right now. Do you have your brother with you?"

"No, sir, I left him out at the farm. I was scared to move him around much, not knowin' how bad he might be busted up inside."

"That was a good idea." Forgetting his coat in his haste, Judah steered the man out of the church. Tied to the hitch rail was a mule that Zeke Fimple must have ridden.

Judah, hurrying to the large stable beyond the parsonage, quickly saddled his horse. He knew he ought to tell Sister Laurel he was leaving, but he did not want to take the time. With Fimple at his side, he rode down Elm Street into the heart of Abilene.

Luckily, Dr. Aileen Bloom was in her office, reading a medical journal in the light of a lantern.

"Hello, Judah," she said with a smile. She looked a bit tired, but as always she was neatly dressed and attractive. Noticing the worried expressions of the minister and the man with him, she frowned. "What's wrong?" she asked.

Judah quickly told her of the attack on Matt Fimple's farm and the beating he had received. The minister had barely finished when Aileen was on her feet, gathering instruments and slipping them into her black bag.

"I'll hitch my horse to the buggy," she said as she snapped the bag closed.

"Let me do that for you, ma'am," Fimple offered.

"All right," Aileen agreed. "The stable is behind the office."

Fimple clapped his hat onto his head and hurried out.

Aileen looked at Judah and said, "You think it was B. W. Royal and his men, don't you? Luke told me about them."

"I'm sure it was Royal," Judah said grimly. "I suppose we should notify the marshal, but I hate to take the time when we don't know how badly they hurt Matt Fimple."

"I'll tell Luke about it when we return," said Aileen as she quickly drew a light shawl around her shoulders. "Let's just get to that farm as fast as possible."

A bright full moon guided the trio across the prairie to the D Slash N. Zeke Fimple led the way, with Aileen's buggy and Judah's horse following closely. Less than an hour after leaving town, the three arrived at a small soddy. The lantern light spilling through the doorway had been visible for several miles.

As Fimple dismounted, a woman ran from the soddy and clutched his arm. "Oh, Zeke!" she cried. "You were gone so long! I was so scared. Matt won't wake up!"

"I got back as soon as I could, Evie," Zeke told the nearly hysterical woman. He put an arm around her shoulders and led her into the cabin.

The words sent a chill through Judah. Had Matt Fimple died from the beating? Judah helped Aileen climb from the buggy, then followed her closely as she hurried into the soddy.

Judah saw the bloody form of a man lying on a rough cot. In one corner huddled four children, three girls and a little boy, who stared fearfully at the newcomers.

Swiftly, Aileen knelt beside the cot, placed her hand against the injured man's neck, and searched for a pulse. Waiting anxiously, Judah stood behind her. After a long moment Aileen glanced up and said curtly, "He's alive."

Judah sighed. Across the room the woman whimpered, and Zeke squeezed her shoulder. "This here's Matt's wife Evie, Preacher. Those kids are their young'uns," he said.

"I'm sure it'll be all right, Mrs. Fimple. Dr. Bloom is an excellent physician," Judah said as he moved to the woman's side and patted her shaking shoulder.

He watched Aileen, who was washing away dried blood and inspecting the wounds, and then he studied the patient. The man had obviously been punched and kicked brutally: One arm lay on the cot at a strange angle, his shirt sleeve tattered and blood-stained, and the unmistakable white gleam of a jaggedly broken bone peeked through the torn sleeve. The anger that had been smoldering inside Judah throughout the long ride to the homestead now threatened to blaze.

Aileen glanced over her shoulder and stated, "I need some help, Judah."

During the next few minutes, Judah repressed his fury and concentrated on assisting Aileen. Matt

Fimple was unconscious, but the pain he experienced while Aileen set his broken arm was strong enough to make him lurch wildly. Judah had to hold him down.

Finally, when the arm was set and splinted, the wounds cleaned, and a long gash on Matt's forehead stitched, Aileen turned wearily to Evie. "Your husband will probably be all right, Mrs. Fimple," she said. "He's not unconscious now; he's asleep. That broken arm is his most serious injury, and I believe it will mend normally."

"Th-thank you, Doctor," Evie replied. She lifted a thin hand and wiped the tears from her eyes.

"He must stay in bed for several days, and he won't be able to use that arm for a long time."

"We'll manage," Zeke said. "I can take care of whatever needs doin'."

Aileen smiled and began explaining to Evie what she needed to do to help her husband recover. The children clustered around their mother's skirts and smiled shyly at the doctor.

Zeke caught Judah's attention. "Can I talk to you outside, Preacher?" he whispered.

"Of course," Judah replied softly, and followed the homesteader.

Outside the earthen cabin in the bright moonlight, Zeke took a deep breath and turned to Judah. "I was afraid poor ol' Matt was done for," he said. "We owe you and that doc a lot."

"Aileen was the one who helped your brother, Mr. Fimple."

"Maybe so, but folks out here know you care. That's more than you can say for most of the people in Abilene."

Judah heard the bitterness and frustration in Zeke's

voice. He told the farmer, "I believe you'll find more people than you think who are glad you and your friends came here. I know they don't show it—"

"You see that?" Zeke asked angrily, gesturing at a dark shape on the ground. "You know what it is?"

Judah was shocked as he recognized it. "It's a cow!" he exclaimed.

"That was our milk cow," Zeke said. "Never hurt nobody, never did nothin' but give milk for the kids. But that didn't stop those no-good raiders from shootin' her down for the fun of it." He swept a hand around him to indicate the fields. "They trampled down all the plants in Evie's vegetable garden and rode through the cornfield. Never saw Evie and the kids so scared. Somebody's got to do something to stop this sort of thing, Preacher! They've just got to!"

Judah nodded bleakly. "I know. All I can tell you, Mr. Fimple, is that we're trying. With the good Lord's help, we will succeed sooner or later."

"When? You ask the Lord that for me, will you?" Zeke snapped angrily. Then he winced and shook his head. "Sorry. I got no call to talk to you like that."

The minister put a hand on his shoulder. "I understand." Suddenly the anger Judah had repressed all evening crept into his voice. "And I am going to do something. I'm not sure what, but it's time for action."

"Mr. Fimple," Aileen Bloom called. "Your sister-in-law wants to talk to you. And I think the children would feel better if you were inside where they could see you. They're very frightened right now."

"Sure," Zeke replied, and hurried into the soddy.

Aileen stood beside Judah. "I heard what you were

saying to that man," she said. "What did you mean by it being time for action, Judah?"

The minister took a deep breath. "The marshal thinks Hunter Dixon hired Royal. Dixon claims to be a Christian. I'm going to go to him as a man of God and appeal to him to put a stop to these raids." The idea had just occurred to Judah, but the more he thought about it, the more it seemed to be the only course he could follow.

"I was afraid you were going to say that. What if it doesn't work, Judah?"

Involuntarily, the minister's slender fingers clenched into fists. "Then I'll go to B. W. Royal himself."

Aileen put a hand on his arm. "You can't do that, Judah. It's too dangerous. The only reason Luke was able to ride into that camp and leave it alive was that they knew he could handle a gun." She smiled warmly at Judah. "You're a fine pastor for your church, but you're hardly a gunfighter."

Slowly Judah opened his hands. Aileen was right, and he knew it. His hands were made for holding a Bible, not a Colt. "All right," he said. "But I'm still going to see Hunter Dixon. I'll go tonight if you think you can manage to go back to town alone."

"I'll be fine," Aileen assured him. "I've been over the trail quite a few times, and that moon is so bright it's almost like day. But I think you should wait before you go to Dixon's. I'm sure Luke or Cody would gladly go there with you."

Judah shook his head. "I don't want to wait. I want to go now while the memory of what those men did here is still so vivid."

Although Aileen continued to try, she could not dissuade him, and a few moments later Judah swung into his saddle and rode toward Dixon's Rafter D range. He had promised her that he would go to the ranch and then return to town.

Judah fervently hoped that by that time he would have taken the first step toward resolving this senseless conflict.

Hunter Dixon stormed onto the front porch of his ranch house holding a shotgun. The cattleman squinted into the moonlit yard and called, "Who the hell's out there?"

"It's Judah Fisher from Abilene, Mr. Dixon," the minister replied as he reined in.

"The preacher? Sorry I cussed at you. I heard someone riding up, but I never figured it'd be you, Pastor."

"Do you mind if I get down, Mr. Dixon? I've been doing a great deal of riding tonight."

"Sure, sure." Dixon opened the door behind him as Judah dismounted. "Come on inside. Can I get you — No, I don't guess you'd want a drink, would you?"

Judah's lips tightened. As a matter of fact, he did want a drink. However, he had put that behind him, and with God giving him strength, he would never allow whiskey to overcome him again.

"No, thank you," he said politely. He stepped onto the porch. "I think we can talk out here just fine."

Dixon frowned at the cool tone in Judah's voice. "Is something wrong, Pastor?"

"There certainly is," said Judah firmly. He took a deep breath. "To put it plainly, Mr. Dixon, I want you to call off the gunmen you hired to drive those settlers off Doyle Needham's land."

"You, too?" Dixon snapped angrily. "You've been talking to that marshal. I told Travis, and now I'll tell you: I didn't bring B. W. Royal to Abilene. But as long as he and his men are here, I'm not going to shed any tears over what they do."

"Even when they kill innocent men?" Judah shot back.

"Those sodbusters knew they weren't welcome here. And I'm damned if I understand why you're taking up for them!"

"They're God's children, just like the rest of us," Judah replied simply. "They have a right to live their lives undisturbed."

"Well, so do the ranchers! We've got a right not to have fences and plows and . . . and . . ." Dixon shook his head. "You don't understand, and I don't think you ever will." He pointed a blunt finger at Judah. "But you're meddling in things that don't concern you. I won't lift my hand to a preacher, but I'll thank you to get off my land."

Dixon's voice had risen in volume, and several of his ranch hands appeared at the bunkhouse door to watch the confrontation.

Judah prayed silently that he could keep a tight rein on his temper. He knew he would regret giving in to his impulse to throw a punch at Dixon. "All right, I'm leaving," he said curtly. "But remember this. You can't run roughshod over this territory forever, Mr. Dixon. Things change all the time, and you'll have to change with them."

Hunter Dixon shook his head. "My way's always been good enough."

Discouraged, Judah realized any further conversation was pointless. He swung onto his horse and turned the animal around. As he rode away, he ignored the ribald comments coming from the bunkhouse. Futile though this visit had been, he knew he could not live with himself if he had not tried to change Hunter Dixon's mind.

And now? he thought. Now, as he had promised Aileen, he would go back to Abilene. Along the way, with any luck, he would shed the ugly anger that threatened to overwhelm him.

Lost in thought, he had been riding toward town for fifteen minutes when the sound of approaching hoofbeats startled him. Judah stopped and tried to determine where the sound was coming from. He turned toward a small rise to the left of the trail just as a rider came over it.

The stranger, upon seeing the minister, reined in suddenly. As the man's hand slid toward the gun strapped to his hip, a cold dread ran through Judah. Then the rider, pistol still holstered, urged his horse closer.

"Good evening," Judah said, his voice firm.

The rider stopped a few feet away from Judah and studied him. "Howdy," he said after a long moment. "You're that preacher from Abilene, aren't you? I just came from there."

"I am."

"What are you doing on my pa's land?" the stranger asked harshly, and Judah realized he must be Brice Dixon. Studying the young features in the moonlight, Judah recognized him.

"I've been to see your father," he said.

Brice laughed scornfully. "Never knew Pa to be much for preaching."

"I asked him to stop the violence that's plaguing the community," Judah said tightly. "Those masked night riders badly injured another man tonight. Thank God he wasn't killed like Ed Morton."

"You're mighty concerned about those sodbusters, Fisher. What the hell have you got to do with them?"

"I don't like to see anyone hurt. It doesn't matter to me what they do for a living."

"Real compassionate, aren't you?" Brice's tone grew uglier. "Seems to me you're showing more compassion for outsiders than for the folks who've lived here for years. They're nothing but a bunch of damned squatters!"

"They're not hurting anyone," Judah insisted. "They're working that land with Needham's permission."

"And what happens next? More farmers show up and ruin this land for cattle, that's what happens." Brice spat contemptuously.

"There's no point in this conversation," Judah snapped. "I'll pray for you, Brice, pray that you'll learn to understand your fellowman." Rigid with anger, the minister spurred his horse and rode past the young man.

Brice's mocking laughter followed him. "You go right ahead and pray, Fisher. But sooner or later you'll figure out that prayer doesn't mean a thing unless it's backed by lead."

The harsh words stung Judah. He had always hated violence. Violence had taken his father, and his brother's job as a deputy frequently put him in danger. But deep down, a part of Judah feared that Brice Dixon was right. Maybe bullets did accomplish more than prayer. . . .

Judah shook his head. His faith was too strong to be shaken by a few insults from an arrogant young cowboy who had probably spent the evening in town guzzling cheap whiskey.

Suddenly, Judah frowned. He stopped his horse and peered over his shoulder. Brice was gone, no doubt heading back to the ranch house. He had said that he was returning from Abilene, and yet he had not been on the usual trail. He had come instead from an area to the southeast, which was unfamiliar to Judah.

Puzzled, Judah turned and walked his horse to the place where he had confronted Brice. He dismounted and led the animal to the top of the rise where Brice had first appeared. By squinting in the moonlight, he saw a narrow, twisting trail.

After a moment's thought, Judah climbed into the saddle, compelled by the curious impulse to know where Brice Dixon had been. Riding slowly and bending so he would not lose sight of the path, he urged the horse down the moonlit trail. Ten minutes later, he spotted a campfire through the trees.

Judah breathed a short prayer. He had told Aileen that he might have to pay a visit to B. W. Royal, but he had not really expected it to happen. Now, he realized, it had. He rode boldly into the camp, ignoring the men who sprang from their bedrolls and pointed pistols at him.

"I want to see B. W. Royal," he announced in a loud voice as he stopped his horse near the campfire. The words boomed loudly around the clearing, just as they did when he preached his sermons in church.

A buck-toothed man thrust the barrel of a gun at him and demanded, "Who the hell are you, mister?"

Judah glanced down at himself. He was not wearing a coat or tie or hat, and he was sure he did not look like a preacher. Probably the only reason none of these hard-faced men had fired at him was that he appeared harmless. With his slender build and wire-rimmed spectacles, he knew he did not look like much of a threat to anybody.

"My name is Judah Fisher. I'm the pastor of the Calvary Methodist Church in Abilene. I'd like to speak to B. W. Royal, please."

"Well, I don't know if B. W. wants to talk to some preacher—" the buck-toothed man began.

A big, bearded man thrust back the entrance flap of the largest tent. "That's enough, Wylie," he growled. "I'll be glad to talk to the preacher. What can I do for you, Reverend Fisher?"

Judah took a deep breath. "I've come to ask you to stop terrorizing the settlers on Doyle Needham's land. I saw what you did to Matt Fimple tonight, and it was the work of monsters!"

"Riding in here and calling folks bad names isn't a very Christian attitude, Reverend. I don't know this Fimple you're talking about." Royal smiled arrogantly.

"And I'm sure you didn't know Ed Morton, either," Judah replied coldly. "But that didn't stop you from gunning him down."

"We ride where we please." Royal's voice hardened. "And if anybody tries to stop us, we're not to blame if something happens. This was meant to be open range, Preacher. We intend to keep it that way."

"Because that's what you're being paid to do," Judah said.

Royal smiled again. "The laborer is worthy of his hire. Isn't that what it says in the Bible, Preacher?"

Judah swung from the saddle and stepped toward Royal. The red glare from the campfire shone on his spectacles as he said angrily, "I won't have you perverting the word of God to justify your evil. I insist that you leave this area!"

Royal jabbed a blunt finger into Judah's chest. "And what if we don't? Are you going to pray down a plague of locusts or some other Old Testament vengeance on us? I've read the Good Book, too, Fisher. God helps those who help themselves, remember? What can you do?"

Weeks of pent-up anger and frustration suddenly boiled over. Without thinking, Judah balled his fists and swung at Royal's smirking face.

The big man moved lazily to the side, letting the wild punch go past his grinning face. Then he stepped closer and slammed a fist into Judah's middle.

Pain exploded in Judah's belly. He staggered backward, clutching at himself. Bile burned in the back of his throat, but before he could react, Royal swung a roundhouse right to the minister's jaw.

Crashing onto his back, Judah felt all the air rush out of his lungs. As he lay on the ground, gasping for breath, he heard Royal laugh. "He's all yours, boys," the leader shouted. "Enjoy yourselves, but don't kill him."

The men moved in around Judah and yanked him to his feet. His wobbly legs were like putty, but the outlaws took turns holding him up while they beat him. After the first few punches, he hardly felt the blows. By the time they let him slump to the ground and began stomping him with their boots, he was floating in a sea of numb shock. The kicks were mere jolts, nothing more.

Finally, a distant voice snarled, "That's enough. I've heard this preacher is a friend of that sodbuster Parks. Take him there and leave him. Maybe this will teach Parks a lesson."

Rough hands reached for him through the hazy shadows that surrounded him. The shadow hands gripped him, pulling him toward the enfolding darkness. He went willingly. . . .

In the dimly lit earthen cabin, Tommy and Verna slept deeply, Tommy on his cot in one corner, Verna on hers in another, which she had curtained off with an old blanket. A single candle flickered beside Isaac, who sat at the plank table fitfully trying to read. Benjamin Franklin's autobiography, the only book Isaac owned other than the Bible, lay open in front of him. He had read the same passage repeatedly, but the words had no meaning.

It had been another long day of backbreaking work, one more in an endless line of such days. But Isaac had chosen this life for himself and his family, and he would not trade it for any other. But, Lord, it made a man tired.

Isaac's eyes were drooping closed when the sound of hoofbeats outside startled him. Guns blasted, and men whooped. Tommy leaped off the cot, looking around wildly and grappling for the rifle that lay on the floor beside his bed.

"Here's a present for you, sodbuster!" a man's voice snarled.

There was a thump near the doorway, then the sounds of retreating hoofbeats, shooting, and yelling. Isaac glanced warily at Tommy. Poking her tousled head from behind the hanging blanket, Verna, eyes wide with fear, exclaimed, "Tommy! What is it?"

"Don't know, Verna," Tommy replied in a hoarse whisper. "But I want you to get back in that corner and stay down."

"Please do as he says, child," Isaac said firmly. He reached for his shotgun, which rested on pegs hammered into the wall, and took it down. He then blew out the candle, plunging the soddy into darkness. Tommy slipped beside him, and together they slowly approached the door. With the barrel of his rifle, Tommy thrust the canvas flap aside. In the silvery moonlight, they saw a huddled dark form, lying on the ground a few feet from the soddy doorway. "My God!" Isaac cried. Heedless of any possible ambush, he rushed to the groaning body and bent over the injured man.

Tommy hurried after him and scanned the moonlit prairie for any intruders. There was no sign of anyone.

Isaac knelt beside the body and gently turned it over. He gasped when he recognized Judah Fisher's bloody face bathed in moonlight.

"It's Judah, and he's hurt bad, son. Help me get him inside."

Laying their weapons on the ground, the two men lifted Judah and carried him gingerly into the soddy. As they moved inside, Isaac told Verna to relight the candle. The guttering flame caught a moment later, casting a feeble glow in the room. Verna groaned when she saw Judah.

They eased him gently onto Tommy's cot. "We'll need some hot water," Isaac said to Verna, and she hurried to the stove to stoke the fire. Tommy went outside to retrieve the rifle and shotgun, while Isaac stood over the cot, peering thoughtfully at the unconscious minister. As the young man returned, Isaac gripped his arm.

"I want you to ride to Abilene," he said. "Find Luke and Cody and tell them what's happened to Judah. You'd best bring Dr. Bloom back with you, too."

Tommy nodded. "You think those varmints who did this will be back?"

"Not tonight. They've already done what they came to do. Get going, son. I don't know how badly hurt Judah is, but I think he needs medical attention."

"I'll be back as quick as I can," Tommy promised. Grasping the rifle, he left the soddy to saddle his horse. A few moments later, as Verna carried a basin of hot water to the cot to clean Judah's wounds, the thunder of hoofbeats rang clearly in the cabin.

Isaac, a terrible fury glittering in his eyes, turned from the cot and picked up the shotgun from the table where Tommy had placed it. "Do what you can for him, girl," he said to Verna.

She glanced over her shoulder in alarm. "Where are you going, Isaac?"

"The moon is so bright I can follow the tracks of those men," he said grimly. "I'm going to go see the man who did this horrible thing."

"Isaac—no. . . !" Verna's plea rang in the cabin, but Isaac had already gone. She could not run to stop him. Judah Fisher needed all of her attention; he was in terrible shape.

On the rise behind the soddy, a man sat on horseback, watching Isaac Parks ride away. He was still and quiet until the old man had disappeared into the night.

Then the rider nudged his horse.

Chapter Thirteen

LUKE TRAVIS, AFTER COMPLETING HIS NIGHTLY ROUNDS, was opening the door to the marshal's office when he heard thundering hoofbeats cross the bridge over Mud Creek at the western edge of Abilene. A galloping horse was not uncommon, but at this time of night the urgent sound made Travis turn in the doorway and peer down Texas Street.

"What is it, Marshal?" Cody asked. The deputy was sitting behind the desk with his feet propped up.

Travis shook his head. "Don't know. But whoever that is, he's in a big hurry." Swinging his feet off the desk, Cody stood up and moved toward the door.

As the galloping horse and its rider flashed through a patch of light from one of the saloons, Travis exclaimed, "It's Tommy Parks!" He hurried to the edge of the boardwalk.

"Then there's trouble," Cody said as he strode onto the boardwalk and stood next to Travis.

Tommy hauled his horse to a staggering stop in front of the marshal's office. The animal's sides were heaving, and foam flecked its mouth. Tommy dropped from the saddle.

"You—you've got to come, Marshal," he gasped as he rushed to the boardwalk. "We need the doctor, too."

Travis gripped Tommy's arm. "Take it easy, son," he said. "We'll get the doctor. Just tell us what happened."

Tommy looked at Cody for a moment, then said, "It's your brother, Deputy. He's been hurt bad."

"Judah?" Cody caught his breath. "What happened to him? Who did it?"

Travis glanced sharply at Cody, then turned back to Tommy. Still breathless and panting, the young man said, "It was those night riders. They came ridin' up to the soddy, shootin' and howlin', and dumped poor Judah's body on our doorstep. He's been beat up awful bad."

"But he's alive?" Travis asked.

Tommy nodded. "He was when I left. And I made good time gettin' here."

An angry curse exploded from Cody. His horse was tied to the hitchrack in front of the office, and before either Travis or Tommy knew what he was doing, he had vaulted the rail and grabbed the saddle horn.

"Wait a minute, Cody!" Travis shouted as the impulsive young deputy swung into the saddle.

"Wait, hell!" Cody was hatless, but he was wearing his gun. He dug in his spurs and raced down Texas Street.

Travis bit off a curse. Turning to Tommy, he asked,

"You don't actually know what happened to Judah, do you?"

"No, Marshal, we don't. But I know who brought him to our cabin, and that's enough for me."

"For Cody, too," Travis muttered as he stepped off the boardwalk and hurried to his horse. Cody had already disappeared. If he got much more of a lead, Travis knew he would not catch him.

He had told Cody where B. W. Royal's camp was located. Unless the gang had changed campsites—which was unlikely since they had protection on Hunter Dixon's land—Cody would be able to find them. Given Cody's rage, Travis was certain there would be gunplay, but as good as Cody was, he would be no match for a camp full of hired gunmen.

Travis jerked his mount's reins loose and hurtled into the saddle. As he wheeled the horse around, he said to Tommy, "Go on down to Dr. Bloom's office and bring her to your place. Tell her what you told us about Judah."

Tommy nodded. "Where are you goin', Marshal?"

"To try to keep Cody from getting himself killed," Travis answered.

Verna knelt beside the cot and dabbed a wet cloth on Judah's forehead. Tiredness gripped her, but she felt as if she would never sleep again. She was too frightened, too worried about all of them—Judah, Isaac . . . and Tommy.

In the time since Isaac had left, she had cleaned the scratches on Judah's face and stanched the flow of blood. His features were bruised and swollen, and as she bathed his face, he softly moaned. He had not yet opened his eyes. Verna could not tell if he even knew where he was.

The minister's chest rose and fell rhythmically. Verna had examined him as best she could, and as far as she could tell, he had no broken bones. He would probably be all right once he had had some time to rest.

A footstep crunched heavily in the doorway, and the canvas flap covering the entrance swished as it was pushed back. Verna gasped in surprise and started to turn around. She had not heard a horse come up to the soddy, but she supposed that Isaac or Tommy had returned for some reason.

Instead, Brice Dixon lounged in the doorway, an arrogant grin on his face. "Evening, girl," he said as Verna lifted a clenched fist to her mouth. "Looks like the menfolk left you all alone to play nursemaid to that preacher."

Drawing a deep breath, Verna forced herself to lower her hand. She might be afraid, but she refused to let this young man know it.

"Isaac and Tommy will be back soon," she said, hoping her voice would not betray her panic. "They've just gone to fetch the doctor for poor Reverend Fisher."

Brice stepped into the cabin and moved toward the cot. There was curiosity on his face but absolutely no concern as he studied Judah's battered features. "Doesn't look to me like he's going to be waking up anytime soon. That means we've got some time to ourselves, doesn't it, Verna? That's your name, isn't it, gal? Verna?"

She nodded jerkily. "Th-that's my name. You'd

better leave now, Mr. Dixon. You don't want to go disturbing the reverend."

Brice laughed. With a smirk on his lean face, he said, "Oh, no, we sure don't want to disturb the reverend."

Verna knew enough not to relax, but still she was startled by his next move. He lunged, and as he grabbed her, his fingers dug cruelly into her arms. Pulling her close to him, he whispered savagely, "Since we don't want to bother anybody, you'd best not yell too much, gal. But you can fight some if you've a mind to. I'd like that."

Verna struggled to jerk away, but he was too strong. As fear flooded through her, her self-control deserted her, and she screamed in terror. Her cry was stifled abruptly when Brice Dixon roughly pressed his mouth over hers.

As he kissed her, she pounded her fists futilely against his back. When she finally thought to knee him in the groin, he was already prepared for the move. Turning away sharply, he took the blow on his thigh, nevertheless grunting in pain.

Brice tore his mouth from hers. As Verna gasped for breath, he viciously slapped her face. Before she could react, he hit her again with a backhand. With a nasty grin, he sneered, "Of course, I never promised I wouldn't fight back."

Stunned by the slaps, Verna swayed numbly. With his left hand Brice gripped her tightly, and hooking the fingers of his right hand in the collar of her nightdress, he savagely yanked at the thin cotton. The fabric ripped with a shredding sound, and buttons popped to the floor. Verna screamed while he tore the dress again. He had bared one of her breasts, and tightening his embrace, he cupped the soft flesh. Sobs racked Verna's body; she knew all too well what the next few minutes would bring. Locked together by Brice's lust, the two of them staggered toward the soddy wall.

The back of her thighs hit the edge of the table. Brice, lost in his own desires, continued to rip at her nightdress, unaware that she had steadied herself. Desperately, as Verna's hand flailed behind her, her fingers fell on something that her numbed brain recognized as the handle of a frying pan.

Acting reflexively, she snatched the pan and whipped it wildly toward Brice Dixon's head. She would have killed him then if she could, would have battered his head with every ounce of energy she possessed. But she was a fraction of a second too slow. Brice raised his right arm as he glimpsed the pan coming at him, and as the heavy iron pan thudded into his forearm, he cried out in pain.

"Stop it!" he shouted, shoving Verna away from him. "Drop that pan, gal!"

Overwhelmed by fear and anger and hate, Verna did not heed his warning. She lifted the pan and started to lunge at him.

Behind Brice, on the narrow cot, Judah Fisher opened his eyes. He had heard muttering for what seemed like hours. His pain-fogged mind could not understand the words, and he did not know how long he had been drifting toward consciousness. But the screams and cries had pierced the fog and jarred Judah from the peaceful darkness into the horrifying real world.

Fully conscious, he clearly saw Brice Dixon yank his

gun from its holster and slash Verna Sills with it. How he had gotten to the Parks farm—what role Brice Dixon was playing in this—were questions Judah could not answer.

But he saw Brice's gun slam into the side of Verna's head, then heard metal crack cruelly into flesh and bone. Verna crumpled to the floor as the frying pan clattered away.

His back to Judah, Brice Dixon stood motionless, as if stunned by what he had done. Beyond him Judah saw the limp body of the young woman.

Seeing Verna struck down so brutally galvanized Judah, and somehow he found the strength to get up from the cot and take Brice by surprise. He tackled the young man, wrapping his long arms around him and grappling for the gun.

Despite the fury that had driven him to this desperate act, Judah was extremely weak, and when Brice rammed an elbow into his midsection, the blow dislodged his grip. Then Brice, spinning around, grabbed Judah's shirt and flung him to the floor.

Breath rasping in his throat, Brice stared at Judah's slumped form for a long moment. He shook his head and aimed the pistol at the minister. "Can't leave any witnesses," he muttered.

Judah looked up to see the barrel of the gun pointing at him. He clambered to his knees and tried to struggle to his feet, but his muscles betrayed him. All he could do was stare in disbelief—

The gun blasted, flame darting from its muzzle. The slug slammed into Judah's side, the impact spinning him around and causing him to fall heavily. He could taste the dirt of the hard-packed earthen floor as waves of fiery pain emanated from his side.

Moving like a man possessed, Brice tore around the cabin, overturning furniture and shoving it to the center of the room. He knocked over two oil lamps and spilled the fuel in puddles on the floor. There was a book and some old papers in a chest. Brice tore them out, shredding them as he did, and threw them around.

When he was satisfied, he backed toward the door and glanced around the cabin. Verna had not moved since she collapsed from the blow on the head, and Judah's struggles had grown more feeble. Brice did not care that the preacher was still alive, since he knew that Judah would never have a chance to testify against him. To cover his trail, Brice intended to erase all proof of what had happened.

Reaching into his pocket for a match, he found a lucifer, flicked it to life, and waited until it was burning strongly. Then he tossed the match into a puddle of lamp oil.

The littered paper caught quickly, followed by bright blue flames leaping from the pile of wooden furniture. As the fire spread, Brice ran from the cabin. He raced to his horse and mounted. For one long moment he looked at his handiwork and smiled. A garish red glow lit the soddy's doorway, and sparks flew to the thatched roof.

Still grinning, Brice dug in his spurs and galloped across the moonlit field toward his father's ranch.

Inside the soddy, the crackling flames, smarting fumes, and searing heat overcame Judah Fisher's pain. Blinking against the smoke, he struggled onto his hands and knees and began crawling across the floor. Verna lay somewhere in front of him, he hoped.

Or rather, he prayed, because he knew that divine help was needed. Beaten and shot, he had little strength left. The Lord would have to provide for them now.

He touched Verna's ripped dress. Sliding his arms around her, he braced himself and pushed against the floor. It was a long nightmare of smoke and flame and heat, a vision of hell more vivid than Judah or any preacher could conjure up in a sermon.

As the fire gutted the inside of the soddy, the two limp forms somehow tumbled through the door and into the cool night air. Judah pulled Verna a few feet farther from the flames, then collapsed beside her. Reaching out with a shaking hand, he touched the softness of her throat. He found a pulse beat, somewhat erratic but still strong.

Judah closed his eyes and moved his lips in a silent prayer of thanks. He had no idea what would happen next, but for the moment, both of them were alive. . . .

Clinging to that thought, he slipped into the darkness again.

Chapter Fourteen

GALLOPING NORTH OVER THE MOONLIT PRAIRIE TOWARD Hunter Dixon's ranch, Isaac Parks trembled with rage. He knew where the Rafter D was, and he would force the cattleman to tell him where he would find B. W. Royal. Despite the dangers he faced, Isaac could no longer stand by meekly and watch as men like Judah Fisher were brutally beaten. He had always been a peaceable man, but the time had come to change.

Ten minutes after leaving his soddy, Isaac reached the trail that led from Abilene to Hunter Dixon's ranch. As he veered onto it, the faint sound of a gunshot startled him. Frowning, he reined in and peered into the night behind him.

It sounded as though the shot had come from his cabin. If so, someone else must be there now, because Verna and Judah had been alone when he left.

A choking sensation seized Isaac, and he recognized

it as fear. Every instinct told him that something was very wrong. A moment later, a faint red glow lighting the sky confirmed his horrible suspicions.

Yanking his mount around, Isaac heeled it to a gallop. As he drew closer to the cabin, the red glow became brighter, and he knew with a chilling certainty that the place was on fire. He whispered a short, heartfelt prayer.

As Isaac raced toward home, his coat flapping in the wind and tears streaming down his cheeks, he suddenly spotted someone riding toward him. The man galloped down the trail at breakneck speed, as if he were fleeing something.

Maybe he was running from the fire at the soddy, Isaac thought as he hauled back on the reins and brought his horse to a sliding stop. The other man was close now, pulling on his own reins and causing his mount to rear and paw at the air. As the two men stared at each other across several yards of ground, the bright moonlight shone clearly on the other man's face—Brice Dixon.

"You!" Isaac exclaimed. He knew how Brice hated them, remembered in a flash that he had tried to molest Verna.

His brain screaming a warning, Isaac started to raise his shotgun. He was too late.

Brice jerked his Colt from its holster and triggered twice. The first shot was hurried, the wild slug kicking into the dirt in front of Isaac's terrified horse, but the second found its target. The bullet slammed into Isaac's chest, killing him instantly. Tumbling from the saddle, his body thudded to the ground.

The gun trembled in Brice's hand as he shook with fear. To calm his shattered nerves, he slowly holstered his gun and drew a long, deep breath. Even if the old man had not trained the shotgun on him, he would have had to kill Isaac Parks. With two murders already behind him, Brice Dixon could not afford to make a mistake. No one could know that he was near the scene of the crimes committed tonight.

Isaac was dead, and with any luck Brice would not meet anyone else on the trail. Once he reached the Rafter D, he would be safe. All the ranch hands would swear that he had never left the place that night.

Leaving Isaac's body sprawled on the moonlit trail, Brice Dixon spurred his horse toward home.

Luke Travis needed all the speed his horse could possibly give to catch Cody. Fueled by pent-up fury, the deputy was galloping recklessly toward Hunter Dixon's ranch. In the bright moonlight, Travis knew Cody would easily find the side trail that led to B. W. Royal's camp.

When Travis finally spotted Cody riding ahead of him, he called to the young man to wait. Cody slowed a little, and Travis quickly pulled up beside him. The marshal leaned over, grasped the reins of Cody's horse, and pulled the animal to a stop.

"Dammit, Marshal, why'd you do that?" Cody demanded angrily.

"So you'd stop long enough for me to talk some sense into that hard head of yours," Travis shot back. "What were you planning to do, have a shoot-out with twenty men?"

"I've faced tough odds before," Cody snarled arrogantly.

Travis nodded. "I know it. But you didn't have a choice then, and, if you remember, you almost got yourself killed. You know you can't ride into Royal's camp with guns blazing. That won't help Judah or anyone else."

The truth of Travis's words made Cody stop. The deputy took a deep breath, and after a moment he said, "Maybe you're right."

"Of course I am. We'll both go see Mr. B. W. Royal."

Cody suddenly grinned. "Sounds like you have a few scores to settle yourself."

Travis grinned and urged his horse to a trot. "Come on," he called over his shoulder. As his deputy drew even with him, the marshal spurred his horse to a gallop.

A few moments later they heard the drumming of fast hoofbeats behind them. Glancing over his shoulder, Travis spotted a lone rider following them. "Wait a minute," he called to Cody. "Who's that?" The lawmen pulled their horses to a halt.

As the horseman pounded toward them, both lawmen rested their hands on their guns. The rider suddenly called out, "Wait up, Marshal!"

"That's Tommy Parks," Cody said in surprise. "You told him to take the doctor to his place to help Judah."

"Something else must be wrong," Travis said with an anxious frown.

Tommy reached them a moment later. The young man patted the exhausted animal's sweating neck and said, "I couldn't find the doctor anywhere in town, Marshal. Didn't know what to do, so I thought I'd best come after you."

Travis frowned. "Aileen should have been either in her office or the room she rents. Did you check there?"

"Yes, sir. Mr. McCarthy showed me where it is."

Tommy shook his head. "There's just no sign of her, and nobody's seen her, either."

"She must have had an emergency call," Travis said thoughtfully. He glanced at Cody. "Do you want to go to Royal's camp or the Parks farm?"

Cody's jaw tightened. He asked Tommy, "You said Verna and your pa are looking after Judah?"

"That's right. But I don't know how badly he's hurt."

"You'd better go to the cabin," Cody decided. "We'll go to Royal's. When you know how Judah is, go back to Abilene. If Aileen hasn't returned, get Orion to help you find Dr. Wright. That's the retired doctor."

Agreeing with Cody's suggestions, Travis and Tommy rode side by side with the deputy. The trail that led to Needham's spread and beyond to Dixon's ranch was easy to follow, and Travis knew that even at night he could find the smaller path to Royal's camp once they reached it. As they passed the turnoff for Needham's ranch, Tommy swung his horse onto the smaller trail and waved a hand in farewell. Travis and Cody continued on.

They had gone less than a hundred yards when they heard Tommy Parks utter a hoarse shout.

"What's the matter?" Cody asked, pulling his horse to a stop and looking back.

"Looks like Tommy's found something. Come on."

They cut across a field, not sticking to the trail. Up ahead, they could see Tommy's horse and a second mount. Tommy was kneeling on the ground beside a dark shape, and as Travis and Cody drew closer, the marshal felt a terrible sense of dread.

"No," Travis breathed as he and Cody reined in.

"It's Pa," Tommy said as he looked up from the body. His voice was thick and choked with emotion.

Travis dismounted and examined Isaac Parks's body in the moonlight. "Shot in the chest," he said. "Just one shot, from the looks of it. God, I'm sorry, Tommy."

Tommy, grief and rage blending on his stricken face, stood up abruptly. "It was Royal!" he howled. "Royal and his damned hired thugs! They killed him!"

Travis felt his eyes grow moist, and he frowned as he looked at the furious young man. He knew the kind of man Isaac had been, knew that Isaac would have wanted to confront Royal about Judah's beating. Perhaps Isaac had been heading for Dixon's ranch to start his search for the outlaw leader there. Unfortunately, at the moment they had no proof that Royal had had anything to do with Isaac's killing.

"Just hold on, Tommy," he began. "We'll get to the bottom of this. We'll find whoever killed your pa—"

"You know damn well it was Royal!" Tommy snapped. He turned toward his horse.

"Wait a minute, Tommy!"

Ignoring Travis, the young man leaped onto his horse and banged his heels on its flanks. As the animal bounded into a gallop, Tommy yelled bitterly, "I'll kill him myself!"

Travis hurried to his horse and mounted up. "We've got to go after him. You think he knows where Royal's camp is?"

Cody shrugged. "You told me, I told Judah, Judah could have told him. They've become pretty good friends. Marshal, if he goes busting in there, they'll kill him."

Travis nodded grimly. "I know. He's as hotheaded as somebody else I know. Come on."

The two lawmen galloped after Tommy. It bothered Travis to leave Isaac's body where it had fallen, but there was no time to do anything else right now. Besides, he believed that Isaac would want him to do everything in his power to see that Tommy did not get himself killed. And that was what would happen if Tommy got to Royal's camp ahead of them.

Aileen Bloom had worried about Judah Fisher's visiting Hunter Dixon all the way back to Abilene. When she reached Elm Street, she turned the buggy north toward the Calvary Methodist Church. She would check with Judah first, make sure he was all right, and find out if he had reported Matt Fimple's beating to Luke Travis.

The injured man had been resting quietly when she left the soddy. She was confident that he would recover, given the time to rest and heal. With his brother Zeke, Evie, and the children, the farm work could continue until Matt was on his feet. The family had been lucky.

For now, Aileen thought grimly. It was only a matter of time before the raiders struck again. They brought their grief and suffering to all of the families struggling to carve a place for themselves on Needham's land. Unless Royal and his men were stopped . . .

Aileen understood the frustration that gripped Luke Travis. He was a good man, a man committed to the ideals of justice and fairness, but he was also a man sworn to uphold the law. As much as he might want to settle this problem with a gun, Luke would exhaust every legal avenue first.

The Methodist church was dark when Aileen drew her buggy in front of it, but a small light was burning in the parsonage. Aileen tied her horse and went to the parsonage door. She knocked softly on it so that she would not awaken the sleeping children inside.

A moment later Sister Laurel opened the door and looked in surprise at Aileen. The Dominican nun held a book in her hand, a finger marking her place.

"Good evening, Sister," Aileen said quietly. "I didn't mean to disturb your reading, but I'm looking for Reverend Fisher."

Sister Laurel smiled. "A visit from you is never disturbing, Doctor. Come in. I'll see if Judah is still awake."

"Thank you." Aileen stepped into the small parlor of the parsonage. A single lamp burned on a table beside an armchair, and she guessed that Sister Laurel had been sitting there. The nun placed her book on the table, then went upstairs where Judah's bedroom was located.

Idly, Aileen picked up the book and glanced at the spine. *Roughing It,* by Mark Twain. She smiled, remembering some of the humorous tales in the book from her own reading of it a couple of years earlier. She would have thought that Mr. Twain's writings were a bit bawdy for a Dominican sister to read, but then Sister Laurel had never completely fit most people's idea of a nun. The doctor recalled a dangerous masquerade when the sister had played a thoroughly convincing madame.

At the sound of Sister Laurel's footsteps on the

stairs, Aileen replaced the book and turned around. A puzzled frown lined the nun's face. "I'm sorry, Doctor," she said, "but Reverend Fisher isn't here. His room is empty, and I can't find him anywhere."

Aileen tensed. That was not the news she had wanted to hear. "That's all right," she said quickly, trying to keep the concern out of her voice so as not to worry Sister Laurel unnecessarily. "I'll speak to him another time."

"Wait, Doctor." Sister Laurel put a hand on Aileen's arm. "I think I know what you're trying to do, but if the reverend is in some sort of trouble, I have a right to know about it. Judah is my friend, too."

"I should have known I couldn't fool you," Aileen said with a rueful smile. Quickly, she recounted what she knew of the night's events.

When Aileen had finished, Sister Laurel shook her head. "That's Judah, always so eager to do the Lord's work and set right all the wrongs of the world. I think you had better tell Marshal Travis about this, Doctor."

Aileen nodded. "That's what I thought. I'll let you know if I find out anything."

"Thank you." Sister Laurel sighed. "I suppose I shall go back to my reading, but I'm afraid Mr. Twain won't seem so humorous now."

Aileen climbed into her buggy and, flicking the reins, urged the mare to a trot. She reached Texas Street a few moments later and turned toward the marshal's office. Before she reached the door, she noticed lamplight pooling on the boardwalk.

When she went inside, she discovered the office was empty. That was strange, Aileen thought as she glanced into the cellblock to make sure Cody was not dozing on one of the cots. The deputy's hat was hanging on one of the pegs by the door.

Puzzled, Aileen walked onto the boardwalk and thoughtfully looked up and down Texas Street. Abilene was quiet. All she heard were the usual sounds of soft music and laughter coming from several saloons —no fights, no gunshots, no pounding hooves. Nevertheless, the sense that something was terribly wrong haunted her.

If anyone in town knew where Travis was, it would be Orion McCarthy. Aileen left her buggy tied in front of Travis's office and hurried across the street. Her quick steps rang on the boardwalk as she went to Orion's Tavern. Passing her own office, she turned in the tavern entrance and pushed through the batwings.

Standing just inside the doors, Aileen saw that several men were clustered around one of the tables, shouting encouragement and exchanging bets on an arm-wrestling match. On opposite sides of the table sat Orion McCarthy and Leslie Gibson, their sleeves rolled up, their elbows placed firmly on its top, their hands locked together. Each man's muscles strained as he strove to pin the other.

Aileen had spoken to Gibson several times since the night of the dance. They had become friends. The big schoolteacher shared many interests with the doctor. Gibson and Orion were also good friends, and Aileen knew that the two evenly matched men regularly enjoyed arm-wrestling competitions.

Tonight, Orion was getting the better of it. Gibson's hand was slowly dipping toward the tabletop. With a mighty groan, Orion threw the last of his strength into the effort, the muscles in his back and shoulders rippling as he drove Gibson's arm to the side. The teacher's hand thumped on the table.

The Scotsman laughed wearily. "Winner and champeen . . . again!" he proclaimed.

"For tonight," Gibson replied, smiling as he rubbed his arm. "Tomorrow night may be a different story." At that moment, he glanced toward the doorway and noticed the doctor standing there. "Aileen!" he exclaimed. "What are you doing here?"

The men standing around the table grabbed their hats as Aileen strode across the saloon. Orion and Gibson stood up, and the tavern keeper said, "Good evening, lass. Wha' kin we do f'ye?"

"I'm sorry to intrude, Orion," Aileen said. "I know you gentlemen like your privacy. But I'm looking for Luke or Cody. Have you seen either of them this evening?"

"No' for several hours," Orion replied. "Might there be some trouble?"

"I'm afraid so."

"Would it ha' anything t'do wi' young Tommy Parks?"

Aileen frowned and shook her head. "Not that I know of. Why?"

"The lad came in here earlier looking f'ye. I dinna know where t'find ye, though."

Aileen had no idea why Tommy would have been looking for her, unless her medical services were required at the farm. What else was going to happen on this warm, pleasant spring evening?

With a deep sigh, she began to tell the men about Matt Fimple's beating and Judah's reaction to it. "He wanted to go to B. W. Royal's camp," she said, "but I thought I had persuaded him not to. Perhaps, after going to Dixon's, he went there anyway."

"Aye, tha' sounds like something tha' the reverend would do," Orion agreed.

"I don't know much about this B. W. Royal fellow," Gibson said, "but he sounds like a rough character. The pastor could get into quite a bit of trouble if he went there alone."

"That's what I'm afraid of," Aileen said.

Orion nodded. "I think I'd best round up a few o' the lads and pay a visit t'yon camp—just t'make sure tha' Judah's all right, mind ye."

"You can find the place?" Aileen asked.

"Aye. Lucas told me 'twas on Dixon's land, near the creeks leading into the Solomon. 'Twill no' be hard t'find."

"I'll go with you, Orion," Gibson said as he rolled down his shirt sleeve and buttoned the cuff.

"And so will I," Aileen declared.

Orion glanced at her sharply and shook his head. "'Tis no place for a woman."

"I'm a doctor first, Orion," Aileen said firmly. "If there's been trouble, my services may be needed."

"She has a point, Orion," Gibson observed.

The Scotsman shrugged. "So be it."

Chapter Fifteen

THE WIND TEARING AT TOMMY PARKS'S GRIEF-STRICKEN face caught the tears welling from his eyes and flung them into the night before they could roll down his cheeks. The young man's emotions were in raging turmoil: anger, hatred, most of all grief. He had not always agreed with his father, but he had loved him dearly.

Now Isaac was gone, struck down by the same evil men who had brought such terror to the new settlement. The need for vengeance filled Tommy, vengeance not only for his father but for Ed Morton and all the others who had been hurt by Royal and his hired guns.

He had only a vague idea of where B. W. Royal's camp was as he galloped over the moonlit, rolling countryside. Suddenly he glimpsed the flickering glow of a fire in a screen of trees along a creek.

Tommy reacted without really thinking. He had no

plan, no idea what he would do once he found Royal and his men. He turned his horse toward the campfire. Guiding the running animal through the trees, he pressed his cheek against its neck. The old rifle was in the saddle boot, but he did not reach for it.

A man clutching a rifle leaped into his path from behind a tree. "Hold it!" the sentry yelled.

Tommy kicked his horse, and the animal lunged, its shoulder slamming into the guard and knocking him out of the way. As the man spun backward, his rifle blasted, but the bullet went wild. In a flash Tommy was past him. The young man thundered into the camp, his eyes dry now and darting from side to side in search of B. W. Royal.

In the bright firelight, men were rolling out of their bedding and stumbling from the tents. Most held guns, but confused by what was happening, they had not begun to fire. Tommy spotted a burly, bearded figure emerging from the largest tent, and he knew that he had found Royal. As the man stared at the onrushing rider, Tommy recognized the burning eyes that he had seen on the night of the dance. *This man led that raid and all the others,* he thought.

Yelling hoarsely, Tommy flung himself at the man from the back of the running horse.

Royal tried to jerk his gun up, but he reacted too slowly. Tommy slammed into him, and both men crashed into the tent, collapsing it. Tommy was on top of Royal, trying desperately to get his hands on the bearded man's throat.

Tommy's fingers finally closed on Royal's thick neck, and the young man squeezed with all his strength. Royal, gasping and choking, slashed at Tommy with the gun that was still in his hand.

The barrel of the pistol thudded into Tommy's skull. His head jerked to the side as bright lights pinwheeled behind his eyes. Then something slammed into his back, and hands caught his shirt and yanked him up and off Royal.

Gasping hoarsely, the bearded man sat up. He watched balefully as his men gathered around Tommy Parks, swinging fists and clubs, their booted feet smacking into the young man's sides. Royal, lifting a big hand to massage his sore throat, rasped furiously, "Kill him! Kill the bastard!"

Tommy groaned and huddled on the ground, trying to draw himself up into a smaller target. But he could not escape the vicious boots, clubs, and fists.

Royal climbed slowly to his feet, rubbing his throat while he watched the brutal display. He slid his gun into its holster and growled, "Finish him!"

One of Royal's men held a thick, gnarled branch. As he lifted it, he shouted, "Stand back!" He stepped forward to bring the club crashing down on Tommy's head.

A gun cracked, the slug punching through the shoulder of the man with the heavy club. The impact drove him to his knees and sent the branch spinning from his hands. He clutched his bloody, shattered shoulder and shrieked in pain, while the other men standing around Tommy whirled to face the new threat.

Luke Travis and Cody Fisher walked their horses into the camp, their guns out and ready. Gun smoke curled from the muzzle of Travis's Colt.

"Hold it!" the marshal snapped. "I'll kill the next man who moves."

The crew of hardcases stood motionless. All of

them had holstered their guns to concentrate on beating Tommy Parks. Travis and Cody were heavily outnumbered, but they had the element of surprise on their side—and their guns were drawn. For the moment the two lawmen were in control of the precarious situation.

Royal glared at Travis. "Mighty big talk, Marshal," he snarled. "You know damn well you and that deputy can't take all of us. You start shooting, and we'll cut you to ribbons."

"I imagine your men will," Travis said coolly. "But you won't live to see it, Royal. I'm putting my first bullet right in your head."

After a tense silence, Royal abruptly threw back his head and laughed. "Damned if I don't think you'd do it!" he said.

"You know I would." Travis kept his gun leveled at the big man. The time for that showdown had finally come, and both of them knew it. "Royal, I'm placing you under arrest for the murder of Isaac Parks."

A perplexed frown appeared on Royal's face. "Parks murdered? What the hell are you talking about, Marshal? I haven't killed anybody."

Tommy was still lying on the ground, hugging his aching middle. At Royal's words, he forced himself to sit up. "You gunned him down, you son of a bitch!" he shouted at Royal.

"We found Isaac's body between here and Needham's place," Travis said coldly. "As far as I'm concerned, you're guilty, Royal, and you're going to hang for it."

Royal stared at the marshal, then exploded, "You're crazy! I didn't kill the old coot, and damned if I'll swing for something I haven't done!" He leveled a finger at Tommy. "There's the man you ought to arrest. He stormed in here and attacked me for no reason."

Cody spoke up. "I think he had a reason. You killed his father."

"I tell you I didn't—" Royal broke off his denial and glared at the lawmen. He said, "I'm damned sick and tired of this. You want me, Marshal, you just go ahead and try to take me in."

Travis glanced around the camp, his face grim but showing no fear. He saw the angry looks on the faces of Royal's men and knew they would like nothing better than to go for their guns.

He looked at Cody. The deputy's features were stony, the knife scar gleaming in the firelight. The barrel of his Colt did not move even the slightest fraction of an inch. Through tight lips, Cody said, "I never did like backing down, Marshal. Especially not to trash like this."

A bleak smile pulled at Travis's lips. "Me either, Cody." He met B. W. Royal's burning gaze and said slowly, "All right, Royal. If that's the way you want it."

A grin broke out on Royal's face. His hand started toward his gun—and froze a split second later, as the sound of many rifles being levered crackled in the darkness around the camp.

As Travis and Cody stared at Royal and his men, knowing it would be deadly to let their attention stray, they heard several horses walking into the camp behind them.

"Appears the two o' ye could use a wee bit o' help, Lucas. Think we'll do?" Orion McCarthy's voice boomed.

Travis glanced over his shoulder and saw the big Scotsman sitting on his horse. The Winchester in his hands was leveled at Royal's men. Flanking Orion were Leslie Gibson and several other men from Abilene, every one of them armed with rifles and obviously ready to use them.

"A dozen more men are in the trees, Marshal," Gibson said. "The odds are a little more even now, so the next move should be up to you."

Travis grinned at the burly schoolteacher. "Thanks, Gibson," he said.

"You should thank Dr. Bloom," the schoolmaster replied without taking his eyes off the men he was covering with his rifle. "She's the one who got us to come out here looking for Judah Fisher."

Aileen, a worried frown on her face, slipped from the trees. Concerned for her safety, Travis glanced at Royal and his men, but the hardcases stood still, well aware of the danger that threatened them. They knew they would be cut down if they went for their guns.

"Hello, Aileen," Travis said. "I should have known you'd have something to do with this."

"Have you seen Judah, Luke? I think he may have come here." Aileen's voice was taut with worry.

"He's at the Parks place," Travis answered. "I know he was here first, though, because he got a bad beating. Royal's men dumped him on Isaac's doorstep."

"My God!" Aileen breathed. "I've got to go see about him."

"That's not the worst of it, Aileen. They killed Isaac Parks."

"I told you, we didn't kill him!" Royal exploded. His face was flushed with impotent anger as he glared at the armed men surrounding his camp. He went on,

"We took care of that preacher, all right—taught him a lesson he won't soon forget. But I haven't even seen Isaac Parks tonight."

"You're a liar!" Tommy shouted as he climbed painfully to his feet. "You and your men have been hidin' behind those masks and makin' life hell for all of us!"

"All right!" Royal flared at him. "Why not? You and the rest of that Southern trash don't deserve any better. We tried to run you off, but you were just too damned dumb to go!"

Tommy clenched his fists and started toward Royal, but Travis's voice stopped him. "Hold it, Tommy!" the marshal snapped. "This is a job for the law."

With an effort Tommy held himself in check.

Travis met Royal's intense gaze and said, "All right, mister. You were saying something about me taking you in."

As Royal stared at Travis, the men who had been standing with him began to back away nervously.

Orion called, "Ye'd best be dropping those guns, lads."

Most of Royal's men complied, carefully unbuckling their gun belts and letting them slide to the ground. They stepped away from the weapons and kept their hands raised. Only two men stood with Royal, a wiry man with buckteeth and a stocky, redheaded hardcase.

A reckless grin suddenly appeared on Cody's lean face. "Three against two," he said. "Those are better odds, aren't they, Marshal?"

"They are," Travis agreed.

"Then why don't we settle this with fists instead of guns?"

Travis grinned broadly. For once he had to agree with his hotheaded deputy. He had been aching for the chance to smash a fist into B. W. Royal.

"How about it, Royal?" Travis asked. "That sound fair to you?"

Royal nodded. "I'll enjoy it," he said with a wolfish grin.

"Drop your guns," Travis commanded. While Royal and his two men did, Travis and Cody holstered their own weapons and unbuckled their belts. Orion walked his horse to the two lawmen and took their belts and holsters. When they were unarmed, they started to swing down from their saddles.

Royal and his men leaped forward the instant that Travis's and Cody's boots touched the ground.

Royal slammed into Travis, knocking the marshal against Orion's horse. The Scotsman hauled on the reins and pulled the animal out of the way. Travis staggered to the side. Royal followed him and smashed a fist into Travis's midsection.

The two other men hurtled at Cody. The deputy avoided the first man's lunge, but when he dodged to the side, he ran right into the second man's fist. The blow knocked him backward, and his feet tangled in one of the bedrolls spread on the ground. Cody lost his balance and went down.

As Cody saw the two men leaping toward him, he lashed out with a foot. The kick knocked one man aside, but the other landed on top of Cody. He gouged at the deputy's eyes with one hand while trying to get the other on Cody's throat. Cody whipped his head from side to side to avoid the clawing fingers and brought his knee up into the other man's groin. The man howled in pain as Cody's knee smashed into its target. After he had grabbed the man's shoulders and thrust him away, the deputy rolled to the side and leaped lithely onto his feet.

Royal was about ready to send another punch into Travis's stomach when the marshal caught the outlaw off guard and threw one of his own. His fist caught Royal in the jaw, but the big man shook his head and shrugged it off. A vicious hook drove into Travis's solar plexus and knocked the air out of him. As Royal bore in, Travis lowered his head, lunged under a wild swing, and butted Royal. Royal's feet were not planted, and he fell backward at the force of Travis's tackle.

Royal twisted as he fell, and somehow Travis lay beneath him. His bearded face contorted with rage, Royal battered Travis's face with his fists, snarling as he did so.

The man Cody had kicked had recovered his balance. He snatched up the club that had nearly been used to smash Tommy Parks and swung it at the deputy. As the weapon whipped toward his head, Cody dodged desperately. Before the other man could swing the thick branch again, the deputy stepped in and peppered his face with short, sharp punches, setting him up for a haymaker, which Cody brought up nearly from the ground. His fist crashed into the man's jaw and sent him flying through the air.

The man landed on B. W. Royal, knocking the bearded man away from Travis. Just as Royal struggled to his feet, the marshal scrambled onto his knees and launched himself across the few feet that separated them. The impact of his fist striking Royal's jaw sent pain all the way up Travis's arm to his shoulder.

Royal's eyes rolled in his head as he fell. Travis sprawled next to Royal's stunned form.

That left one man to deal with, the buck-toothed hardcase whom Cody had kneed a moment earlier. The man had rolled close to the campfire, and even as he clutched at himself with one hand, he used the other to scoop up a burning brand and fling it at the deputy. Cody ducked, letting the torch go over his head, but as he did so the man lunged toward one of the discarded gun belts on the ground nearby, his fingers closing over the butt of the pistol and yanking it out of the holster. He twisted around on the ground and started to raise the gun.

Luke Travis pushed himself onto his hands and knees and dove forward. He caught the man's gun hand and forced it down just as the man jerked the trigger. The gun blasted, and the man screamed. He stared in horror at his bloody boot. The gun slipped from his fingers, and he slumped back in a dead faint.

Cody extended a hand to Travis as the marshal got to his feet. The rest of Royal's men had not moved. They, along with the townspeople from Abilene, had watched the brutal battle. Now Travis stepped over to Royal's body and prodded the big man with his boot. Royal groaned and slowly moved his head from side to side.

"Get up, Royal," Travis said hoarsely. "It's over. You're going to jail, where you belong." The marshal turned to Orion. "You and some of the other men get these three on their feet and take them back to town. Toss 'em in jail, and don't worry about being too gentle with them."

"Aye, Lucas," Orion said with a big grin.

Aileen slipped next to the marshal and put a hand on his arm. "Are you and Cody all right?" she asked anxiously.

"I'm fine, ma'am," Cody answered for himself, smiling broadly as he took his gun belt from Orion and buckled it. "That was a pretty good scrape while it lasted."

"It was," Travis agreed. Assuring Aileen he was fine, he strapped on his own gun. The bumps and bruises he had received would heal on their own. He gestured at the wounded raider. "You'd better take a look at that man. I don't want him bleeding to death on the way to town."

"Of course." Aileen hurried to get her medical bag while Orion, Gibson, and the other men took charge of the prisoners and gathered up their guns.

"What about these men, Marshal?" Gibson asked, gesturing with his rifle barrel at the group of hardcases. "I don't think you've got enough cells in Abilene to hold all of them."

Travis considered the problem for a long moment. Royal would be going to jail, that was certain, and so would the two men who had resisted arrest. The others were guilty of terrorizing the settlers on Needham's ranch, but there was a good chance they would only be fined. It would be impossible to discover who among them had actually killed Ed Morton, but as their leader, Royal would bear the responsibility.

"Keep their guns and their gear," Travis said at last. "They can have their horses, so that they can get out of the territory." He faced the surly gang and raised his voice. "Did you men hear that? I want you to leave

Kansas while you've got the chance. We won't stand for your lawlessness any longer."

Standing behind the marshal, the grim-faced posse confirmed Travis's words with their steady rifles.

Slowly, the hardcases mounted and rode away from the camp. As Travis watched them go, he was relieved and felt a warmth growing inside him—pride in Abilene and its people. It had taken them a while to come around, but tonight the citizens had taken a stand.

Travis turned to Tommy Parks and put a hand on the young man's shoulder. "Things will be different now," he said. "You'll see, Tommy."

"I hope so, Marshal. I just wish my pa . . . that he—"

Travis nodded, but before he could say anything, Leslie Gibson called urgently, "Marshal, you'd better get over here!"

Travis wheeled around and saw Gibson hurrying to assist a man who was staggering into the camp leading a mule. A woman trudged on foot beside him. Isaac Parks's body was slung over the back of the mule.

"Judah!" Cody cried as he ran to his brother. He grabbed Judah's arm as the minister started to sway. Travis rushed over and noticed the dark splotches on Judah's shirt. Gibson took the mule's halter while Tommy pulled Verna into his arms and held her tightly. A blanket wrapped around her covered her tattered dress.

"What happened, Verna?" he asked. "You all right?"

"I'm fine, Tommy, thanks to Judah," she replied. "He saved my life."

Travis called to Aileen as Cody helped Judah stretch out on one of the bedrolls. Even in the flickering firelight, Travis could see that Judah's face was pale, and he was struggling to stay conscious. The others clustered around him while Aileen opened his shirt and began to examine the bullet wound. After a moment, she glanced up at Cody and Travis and said, "I believe it's just a deep crease. He's lost quite a bit of blood, and he's weak from the beating, but he should be all right if we can keep the wound from becoming infected." Taking her bag from Orion, she began to clean the wound.

Judah tried to raise his head. "I . . . I have to tell . . . to tell you—"

"Just lie still, Judah," Aileen cautioned him. "You've been through a lot. You need to rest."

"No!" Judah whispered fiercely. Calling on all his strength, he propped himself up on one elbow. "Th-this is important. Marshal, Brice Dixon did this."

"Brice!" Cody exclaimed.

Travis knelt beside Judah. "All right, Judah, tell me about it. Then you do like Dr. Bloom says and take it easy."

His voice fading in and out, Judah managed to relate the story of Brice Dixon's atrocities at the Parks soddy. "After we got out of the fire, I rested a little and then found that mule and a blanket for Verna. We . . . we started looking for help, but then we found Isaac's body. I . . . I couldn't leave him there. Verna told me that Tommy had gone to town to get you and Cody, Marshal. I thought you might . . . might be here." Judah's fingers clutched at Travis's sleeve. "Brice must have run into Isaac when he was fleeing from the cabin. He thought he had killed us, so he had to . . . to—"

"I understand, Judah," Travis said gently. Carefully, he urged Judah to lie back. "You let Aileen patch you up now. We'll take care of everything else."

Travis stood up. As he did so, B. W. Royal said from behind him, "I told you, dammit! I told you I didn't kill Parks! It was that Dixon pup! He's been the one behind all of this."

Travis turned around to face the bearded man. Royal's hands had been tied behind his back, as had those of his men, and they were waiting to be put on horses and taken to Abilene. Travis stepped closer to him and asked, "Just what is your connection with Brice Dixon?"

Royal snorted. "Hell, he's the one who got in touch with me in the first place and had me and the boys come here. He wanted those sodbusters run off for some reason."

"You weren't working for Hunter Dixon?"

"Never even saw the man," Royal declared.

Travis nodded. A few questions remained unanswered, but a clear picture was beginning to emerge. He looked at Cody and said, "I think we'd better go see Brice Dixon."

Cody glanced at his brother's bloody, battered form. He put his hand on the pearl handle of his Colt and grimaced angrily. "I think so, too."

Chapter Sixteen

AILEEN BLOOM STOOD UP AND SNAPPED HER MEDICAL
bag shut. She had cleaned and disinfected the bullet
crease in Judah's side and then bandaged it. She had
also tended to the cuts and scratches he had suffered
in the earlier beating. Now, the minister's head lay on
the bedroll. His eyes were closed, and he appeared to
be asleep.

Travis turned to Aileen and nodded at Judah. "Can
he travel?" the marshal asked.

"He can make the trip back to Abilene," Aileen
replied. "But he'll need plenty of rest."

"I was thinking about his going to Dixon's ranch
now with Cody and me."

Aileen looked dubious. "I don't know, Luke," she
said slowly. "I don't want that wound to start bleeding
again."

Judah opened his eyes, turned his head, and looked

up at Travis. "I can travel, Luke," he said softly. "I'm sure I'll be all right."

Travis knelt beside the minister. "We could probably manage without you, Judah, but I've been thinking about Brice Dixon. We can charge him with hiring Royal and his men to carry out those raids, but I'd like to see him pay for everything else he's done, not just that."

Judah nodded weakly and said, "I . . . I agree. If someone will just help me up . . ."

Orion stepped forward and lifted Judah to his feet. Aileen stood close by, her forehead creased in a frown. "I'm not sure this is a good idea, Luke," she said.

Judah smiled at her. "I'm all right, Doctor. I want to be in on the finish of this. I want to see Brice Dixon brought to justice."

Cody slipped an arm around Judah's waist and helped him walk to a horse. He grinned and said, "Sort of a vindictive attitude for a preacher, isn't it, Judah? I thought I was the vengeful brother."

"'Vengeance is mine, sayeth the Lord,'" Judah quoted. "But He uses many instruments for that vengeance, Cody."

With the help of Cody and Orion, Judah climbed into the saddle. The mount's owner would double up with another man for the ride back to town.

Travis and Cody swung onto their horses. The marshal said, "All right, Orion, the rest of you can take Royal and his men back to town now. Tommy, you and Verna go with them."

Shaking his head, Tommy looked at Travis. "I want to go with you, Marshal. If Brice killed my pa, I've got a right."

Travis considered it for a moment, then nodded. "Yes, you do. Aileen, will you look after Verna?"

"Of course," the doctor replied. "And as soon as you're through at Dixon's, Luke, please bring Judah into town as quickly as you can."

Travis agreed. With a wave to the others, he rode out of Royal's camp, followed by Cody, Judah, and Tommy.

The grim foursome said little as they rode through the night toward the Rafter D headquarters. Concerned that the ride would drain all Judah's strength, Travis set an easy pace. While they rode, the two lawmen checked their guns, then returned the weapons to their holsters.

When they at last sighted the ranch house, Travis lifted a hand to halt the riders. In a low voice, he asked, "How are you doing, Judah?"

"I'm . . . all right, Luke," Judah answered after a moment. "Just pretty tired. My side doesn't hurt very much, just aches a bit."

Travis nodded. He turned to Tommy and said, "I want you and Judah to circle north around the house and come from behind it. Swing wide, so you won't be noticed. I want the Dixons and their men to pay attention to what's happening at the front of the house. You two stay hidden until you see my signal."

"All right, Marshal," Tommy replied. Travis noticed that the young man's face was drawn and haggard. Even though he was functioning, it was clear that his father's death had hit him hard.

"We'll wait here for a few minutes to give you time to get into position," Travis said.

Tommy and Judah both nodded and then rode off. The moon had begun to set, and although it was somewhat dimmer, the light was still bright enough to guide them.

Ten minutes later, Travis and Cody trotted their horses into the front yard of Hunter Dixon's house. A few lights burned in the main house, but the bunkhouse was dark. Most of the hands were probably asleep.

Travis reined in. Leaning on the pommel of his saddle, he called, "Dixon! Hunter Dixon!"

A couple of minutes passed. Travis heard confused muttering inside the bunkhouse, and then a man, holding a lantern, appeared in the doorway. The front door of the main house swung open abruptly. Light from inside spilled onto the porch and into the yard as Hunter Dixon stepped through the doorway with a shotgun in his hands.

"Who the hell is out here yellin' in the middle of the night?" he demanded. He squinted into the darkness. "That you, Marshal?"

Travis and Cody walked their horses toward the house until they stood in the pool of light. A quick glance at the bunkhouse told Travis that the punchers were coming out and hurrying across the yard to the main house.

"Deputy Fisher and I have a few questions to ask, Dixon," Travis told the rancher.

Dixon stared belligerently at them. "By what right? You don't have any authority here."

"I'm a lawman," Travis said simply. "If I have knowledge of a crime, I've got a duty to go after the criminal."

"Then ask your damned questions," Dixon growled.

"They're not for you. They're for Brice."

Dixon glared again, but he turned his head and bellowed into the house, "Brice! Get out here!"

A moment later, Brice stepped onto the porch. The young man was pale. He swallowed nervously and asked, "What do you want, Pa?"

With the shotgun, Dixon gestured toward Travis and Cody. "These star-packers want to ask you some questions."

Brice glared at the lawmen. "I don't have to answer any questions," he snapped. "I haven't done anything."

"Nobody said you did, boy," Dixon replied.

Travis spoke up. "We just want to know where you were earlier tonight, Brice. That's all."

Brice seemed to relax a little. He hooked his thumbs in his gun belt and said, "I was in Abilene for a little while, then here on the ranch for the rest of the evening. Wasn't I, boys?"

Several of the ranch hands who had gathered around the porch hesitated, then finally nodded. Travis was not surprised. These men were concerned with keeping their jobs and had no idea that Brice might have murdered someone.

"Are you sure you weren't over on Needham's range?" Cody asked in a cold voice.

Brice turned sharply to his father. "I told you they've been hounding me, Pa! There must have been some trouble with those sodbusters again, so naturally these law dogs come after me!"

Hunter Dixon looked intently at his son. "You swear you didn't ride over to Needham's tonight, Brice?"

"I swear it, Pa."

Dixon nodded abruptly. "Then that's good enough

for me." He glared at Travis. "You got the answers to your questions, Marshal. I'll thank you to ride on now."

"It's not that simple, Dixon," Travis said. He looked around the yard at the cowboys surrounding them. Most of the men were armed, and all of them were angry and ready to defend their employer and his son. Unless his plan worked, he and Cody would have a hard time arresting Brice Dixon. Some innocent men would get hurt.

Hunter Dixon scowled at him. "Just what are you really after, Travis?"

"A killer," the marshal answered bluntly.

Brice laughed and shook his head. "He's crazy, Pa!" the young man declared contemptuously.

Fixing his gaze on Brice, Travis smiled. Careful not to spook the nervous cowhands, he slowly lifted his hand and made a small gesture. At the sound of approaching hoofbeats, everyone looked toward the north corner of the house.

Judah Fisher and Tommy Parks rode into the lantern light. His hand reaching across the gap between the two horses, Tommy held Judah's shoulder to steady him. In the harsh light, with his bloody shirt, Judah looked like an apparition from Hell.

Brice Dixon's head snapped around. He stared at the two riders, and his mouth fell open in shock. Staggering back, he pointed a shaking hand at Judah. "You're dead!" he exclaimed. "I shot you, dammit! You're dead!"

An awful silence descended on the ranch yard. Hunter Dixon stared at his son in horror. Finally, in a choked voice, he said, "You shot the preacher?"

Brice suddenly jerked back against the wall. Like a

cornered wild animal, he swiveled his head in fear. "What if I did?" he demanded angrily. "He had it coming, him and the girl and that old man. . . ."

"Isaac Parks," Travis said coldly. "Brice shot him when he was running away, after he shot Judah, pistol-whipped Verna Sills, and then tried to burn them to death!"

"What does it matter?" Brice demanded bitterly. He looked at his father, a desperate plea in his eyes. "Parks was just a squatter, Pa. He didn't mean a damn thing!"

Brice reached out, put a hand on his father's arm, and plucked at Dixon's shirt sleeve.

Dixon tore out of his son's grasp. "Get away from me!" he rasped. "I don't know you anymore, boy! I didn't want those farmers here, but I never wanted anybody killed."

"Brice hired B. W. Royal," Travis told the cattleman. "Royal has already admitted it. He and some of his men are in custody. I imagine they'll tell us the whole story."

Dixon glanced again at his pale, shaking son. "Why, dammit? Why?"

"I thought that was what you wanted, Pa," Brice whined. "I just wanted to show you that I could handle things the way you wanted."

Dixon shook his head. The marshal thought the haggard man appeared to have aged ten years in the last few moments. As Dixon backed away from Brice, he muttered, "I won't protect a murderer, son or no son. . . ."

Travis risked a glance at the Rafter D punchers. All of them seemed to share Dixon's revulsion for Brice's crimes. They would not try to prevent Brice's arrest now.

"It's all over, Brice," Travis said softly. "Drop your gun and get your horse. You're coming with us."

Brice stood with his back against the wall of the house. His chest heaved as he panted. He nervously licked his lips as his eyes darted anxiously from one grim face to another. Travis, Cody, Judah, and Tommy stood silently watching the desperate young man.

"No!" Brice yelled suddenly. "You won't take me!" His hand flashed toward the gun on his hip.

Cody Fisher's draw was a flicker of motion. The gun in his hand roared. Brice crashed against the white wooden siding of the house, and for a moment he seemed pinned to the wall. Then his pistol slipped from his fingers and thumped unfired onto the porch while a thin stream of blood trickled from the black-rimmed hole in his chest. His body crumpled to the porch floor.

Tense and ready, Cody held his gun. Travis had drawn his Colt, but Dixon's cowboys gave no sign that they would cause any trouble. In fact, most of them looked a little sick.

"I'm sorry, Dixon," Travis said.

The rancher stared at the body of his son for a long moment, then slowly drew a deep breath. "Get him out of here," he said. "Get him off this ranch." His face a granite mask, Hunter Dixon turned, strode into the house, and slammed the door behind him.

Chapter Seventeen

BASKING IN THE LATE-AFTERNOON SUN, LUKE TRAVIS
surveyed the scene before him and felt an unusual
sense of well-being. The whole town had come to
Doyle Needham's ranch for this covered-dish supper.
A warm breeze ruffled the brightly colored table-
cloths, and groups of laughing, talking people were
clustered around the food-laden tables, while the
youngsters played merrily among the adults.

Many of the area ranchers and their crews had
joined the citizens of Abilene for this get-together that
was being held belatedly to welcome the Georgia
settlers. As a lawman, Luke Travis was always alert for
trouble, but he doubted that anyone would cause
problems today. Not unless some of the ladies started
to argue about who made the best sweet-potato pie.

A week had passed since the night of fire and blood
that had left Isaac Parks and Brice Dixon dead. At last
things had settled down. In an unusually speedy

display of justice, B. W. Royal and two of his men had been found guilty of attempted murder in the assaults on Judah Fisher and Matt Fimple. They were also convicted on several lesser charges stemming from their campaign of terror against the farmers. The trio had been fined heavily and sentenced to a year in prison. The marshal knew that at this very moment they were on their way to the state penitentiary.

He smiled as he watched Tommy Parks, wearing a solemn but friendly expression, move through the crowd, shaking hands and greeting people. Beside him was Verna Sills, wearing a dark dress, which Aileen had given to her. The two young people were mourning Isaac's death, and the loss could be seen in their eyes. But they were coping with their grief and getting on with their lives. There were already signs that Tommy would take his father's place as the unofficial leader of the community. According to Judah, when enough time had passed, he would perform a wedding for Tommy and Verna.

"It looks as though some good has come from all the violence," Aileen said softly.

Startled, Travis turned and smiled at her. "I didn't hear you come up."

"I wouldn't miss this party for anything. I'm sure there'll be some dancing later on. And Leslie Gibson is quite a dancer."

Travis grimaced. "I'm sure he is."

Aileen lightly touched his arm. "But so are you, Luke Travis, and I'm not going to let you use that old buckshot wound as an excuse again. You're going to dance with me tonight, Marshal. Doctor's orders. You need the exercise."

Travis laughed. Exercise was one thing a lawman

usually got plenty of. Then his expression grew serious. "You're right," he said. "Some good things have happened. Folks were so upset by what Brice Dixon and Royal did that they've stopped thinking about the things that aren't important. These settlers are finally part of the community."

"That's as it should be," Aileen agreed. She suddenly laughed and pointed. "Look at Cody and Orion."

Travis spotted his deputy and the tavern keeper sitting at one of the long tables. The plates both men had in front of them were heaped with food.

"They won't be able to move when they finish all of that," Aileen said, "let alone dance."

"Oh, you'd be surprised." Travis chuckled. "When it comes to dancing with pretty girls, Cody and Orion will find a way."

Travis noticed Judah Fisher hurry across the ranch yard toward them. Though he was recovering well, Judah still moved stiffly. "Luke, look over there," he said. The marshal frowned in concern at the urgency in the minister's voice.

At that moment, an ominous silence fell abruptly over the gathering. Travis followed Judah's gaze and could see why.

Hunter Dixon and some of his ranch hands were riding into the D Slash N yard. The Rafter D punchers were driving several head of cattle in front of them.

Dixon reined in and dismounted. As he walked over to Travis, the crowd parted for him. Cody and Orion had seen him arrive, and they hurried to stand next to the marshal in case trouble developed. Judah, Tommy, and Leslie Gibson drifted over, too, along with Doyle Needham.

Travis stood his ground and met the rancher's level gaze. "Hello, Dixon," he said.

Dixon nodded curtly. "Marshal." He touched the brim of his hat and nodded more graciously toward Aileen. "Ma'am."

"I hope you haven't come to cause trouble, Dixon," Travis said. "These folks are enjoying their party."

"No, no trouble, Marshal," Dixon said, shaking his head. He looked at Tommy Parks and Doyle Needham. "I've come to say I'm sorry. I'm sorry about what happened to your pa, boy, and I'm sorry about all the trouble on your land, Needham. Some of it—hell, a lot of it—was my fault. I'm the one who taught Brice to think the way he did."

Tommy took a deep breath. His features were carefully expressionless as he said, "I think we all choose our own paths, Mr. Dixon. You might've pointed him in the wrong direction, but he's the one who did the killing."

"The boy's right, Hunter," Needham added.

Dixon extended his hand to Tommy. "How about we start mending some fences . . . neighbor?"

Tommy hesitated only for a moment. Then he took Dixon's hand and nodded.

The rancher turned to his men and signaled them to herd the cattle toward him. "These are all good milk cows," he said to Tommy. "I want you folks to have them. You've got plenty of families with youngsters, and those kids'll need milk."

"Thanks," Tommy said. "We all appreciate that." Suddenly, he smiled. "Why don't you stay for supper, Mr. Dixon?"

Dixon returned the smile but shook his head. "Not

today. I don't think I'm ready for any festivities yet. But . . . someday I'd be glad to, Tommy. Someday."

He tipped his hat again and turned to his horse. After he had mounted, his eyes met Travis's for a moment. Then he spurred his horse and rode away.

Travis sighed deeply. Now he was certain that the settlers would have no more trouble from Hunter Dixon. The fences would be mended.

Doyle Needham clapped his hands. "I thought we had a party goin' on!" he called. "Let's get back to it!"

As the sounds of talking and laughing filled the ranch yard once more, Aileen slid her arm through Travis's. "Do you think Abilene can get along without you for a while, Luke?"

"It had better. I still want to see Cody and Orion polish off that food." Travis grinned at her. "And I've got a little dancing to do!"

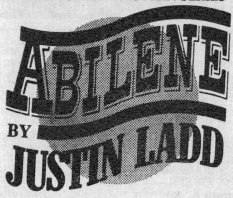